T0082663

The Stockton Saga 6

Mean to the Bone

Steven Douglas Glover

THE STOCKTON SAGA 6
MEAN TO THE BONE

Copyright © 2022 Steven Douglas Glover.

All rights reserved. No part of this book may be used or reproduced by any means, graphic, electronic, or mechanical, including photocopying, recording, taping or by any information storage retrieval system without the written permission of the author except in the case of brief quotations embodied in critical articles and reviews.

iUniverse books may be ordered through booksellers or by contacting:

iUniverse
1663 Liberty Drive
Bloomington, IN 47403
www.iuniverse.com
844-349-9409

Because of the dynamic nature of the Internet, any web addresses or links contained in this book may have changed since publication and may no longer be valid. The views expressed in this work are solely those of the author and do not necessarily reflect the views of the publisher, and the publisher hereby disclaims any responsibility for them.

Any people depicted in stock imagery provided by Getty Images are models, and such images are being used for illustrative purposes only. Certain stock imagery © Getty Images.

ISBN: 978-1-6632-3536-7 (sc)
ISBN: 978-1-6632-3537-4 (e)

Print information available on the last page.

iUniverse rev. date: 02/08/2022

CONTENTS

PREFACE

The *Stockton Saga* began as a short story for a friend. Her positive response encouraged me to write yet another tale of adventure. As others read my stories of gunfighter Cole Stockton, suggestions were made to put them together as a novel. Thus, *The Stockton Saga: Dawn of the Gunfighter* was born. It chronicles his heritage and the elements that formed his mystique.

The stories of Cole Stockton, a man of strong moral character, are infinite. *The Stockton Saga 2: Star of Justice* followed, revealing Stockton's rise to Deputy U.S. Marshal as well as meeting his lady love, Laura Sumner. My bounty of narratives about this man of the law led to *The Stockton Saga 3: A Man to Reckon With*. It continues Cole's encounters in the Lower Colorado Territory during the last half of the 19th Century.

Next, I thought it time to highlight the women of the Old West. *The Stockton Saga 4: The Lady From Colorado* presents lady rancher Laura Sumner in several situations that reveal her strength of character. She encounters danger on several occasions, oversees wranglers as she works alongside them on her horse ranch, and fights for justice for her aging parents. U. S. Marshal Cole Stockton remains a principle character in the novel.

Next, I thought that readers should read more about Cole's younger brother, Clay Stockton and so my next novel, *The Stockton Saga 5: Stockton's Law*, fulfilled my thoughts.

Many of my friends and fans continually ask me when the next Stockton novel is going to be out. This novel, *The Stockton Saga 6: Mean to the Bone*, fulfills requests for more Cole Stockton. Wherever he travels, U.S. Marshal Cole Stockton invokes law, order, and justice.

I try to portray the Old West as it actually was, lending authenticity to the stories. Historical characters have been researched. When I speak of certain weapons, pistol or rifle, they have been researched as well. Smallest details of life and times currency, fashion, food, furniture, and businesses, are each presented as they were in the latter half of the 19th Century.

Continued appreciation goes to my dear friend, Monti Lynn Eastin, for the persona of Laura Sumner. Her support of my writing and continuous prompting me to publish them is genuinely appreciated.

Once again, immense gratitude is given to Gay Lynn Auld for her time and effort editing this manuscript. Her suggestions for expansion proved invaluable.

A special thanks to Linda Glover, without whose review, comments, and moral support this book would not have been published.

Special thanks to my dedicated fans who continue to read my books and keep asking for more.

"The Stockton Saga 6: Mean to the Bone"

I humbly dedicate this book to my son, Steven Douglas Glover Jr.,
who is also one of my most avid readers. Steven, this one is for you.

And to

My wonderful wife, Etta Linda Pybus Glover. She consistently
accompanies me to all of my book signings, ensures that photos
are taken, and that I get that all important cup of coffee to keep
me feeling good while chatting with potential book buyers.

And to

A very wonderful friend, as well as my most
able fantastic editor, Gay Lynn Auld.

And as always

The memory of my most favorite Author, Louis L'Amour
1908 - 1988

CHAPTER ONE

Beyond Bismarck

Johanna Marie Stockton laughed gaily as the Dakota to Denver Stagecoach slid to a whirlwind halt in front of the Bismarck, North Dakota combination stage and express Office.

"Hi Yah, Sammy!" she exclaimed with her beautiful hazel eyes ablaze in the afternoon sun.

The surprised grizzled old driver looked down at her from the driver's box seat with deep admiration.

"Well, I'll be! Johanna! My, you shore are a sight for sore eyes. Now, don't tell me that you are headed back to the Lower Colorado."

"Yes, Sammy, I am. I was hoping that I would find you driving this route."

Sammy Colter fairly leaped down to the ground from the high box with a flair of youthfulness. Immediately, he hopped up onto the boardwalk to stand directly in front of Johanna Stockton and her son, Clay Stockton, who had just joined his mother on the boardwalk.

Sammy shook hands with Clay Stockton, U.S. Marshal for the Dakota Territory, then he turned his utmost attention to Johanna.

"By golly, Johanna, we will have us one heck of a trip. Damn, it's good to see you again."

Johanna blushed. She and Sammy had become fast friends during her first trip from Santa Fe to the Lower Colorado and she felt those stirrings of friendship return. Sammy was quite a colorful character, but he had his soft side also, and Johanna loved the combination.

1

"Well, Johanna, let me check in with Walter, the station agent. We should roll on out of here within the hour. Have yerself ready for a grand ole time."

Johanna laughed, "I'll be ready, Sammy. There's nothing I would like better than to ride your coach."

She then turned to Clay Stockton. Mother and son embraced warmly and said their reluctant farewells.

Sammy returned a few minutes later to check his team, as well as each harness and hook up. The shotgun guard, George Altman, climbed aboard and settled in his seat on the high box. Walter, the station master, assisted Johanna and other passengers to step aboard the creaky coach. Sammy climbed up onto the high box seat and, taking up the reins of his team, he sorted them through his fingers until he felt comfortable that they were right.

Walter signaled Sammy that all passengers were aboard and they were ready to roll.

Sammy glanced down into the coach. He spat his chaw then hollered down. "Hang on, Johanna, and youse other dandies. We are on our way." Sammy cracked his long whip above the team's heads, and yelled his encouragement. "All right now, get up there youse crowbaits. Stretch into them harnesses. Come on now, Sally! Up there, Gordo, lean into it, Sutter! Aw, come on now, you can do better than that, Shadow! That's it Sally! Show them studs how to pull this here coach. Hee Haw."

The coach rocked slightly back and then jerked violently forward. Passengers rocked with the movement of the coach and held on for dear life.

The six-horse team strained into the harness and hooves dug into the earth. Dirt, dust, and pebbles flew backward with the rush and the hostlers as well as the station agent ducked to avoid being hit with flying debris.

"Damn that Colter! Next time I see him, I'll punch him in the nose for this!" yelled Walter.

The coach rocked and swayed down the main street of Bismarck, North Dakota and, once out of town, swerved onto the rutty dirt trail.

Sammy Colter spouted words of encouragement to his team, and the shotgun guard himself held on for dear life.

* *

Nate Culpepper lay on his Omaha, Nebraska hotel room bed with his Colt Revolver at the half cock. He listened intently to the slightly audible "click" of each turn of the cylinder. He was precise in its sound. He was extremely careful to keep it clean and operational.

Nate Culpepper was a gunman. He was not only precise in his work, he was vicious and deadly accurate.

Today, at two o'clock in the afternoon, he was to meet with a man. This man was to pay Nate handsomely for the *execution* of a known figure.

A soft knock came at the door. Culpepper slipped his five foot, eleven inch solidly-built frame slowly off the bed and, with revolver in hand, beckoned his caller to enter.

"I'm looking for Nate Culpepper," said the man dressed in suit and tie.

"You've found him. What is it that you want?"

"I represent an organization with considerable influential backings. If you are interested, I am prepared to offer you five thousand dollars to kill a man."

Nate Culpepper laughed inwardly. His adult life had been given to wasting men for money. He was a fast draw. He was sure of himself. He was extremely vicious and actually enjoyed hunting down and killing men.

Culpepper looked intently at the man before him. This offer was as most of his "dealings." Someone would offer him a goodly sum of money to eliminate someone of importance. The name was of no consequence. Nate would find a way.

The thought formed in his mind that whoever this target was, he was important enough to this organization for them to pay the sum of five thousand dollars. Past targets brought only one to three thousand.

This deal suggested someone who was so good with firearms that the hiring organization had to pay a good price to have him eliminated.

Nate Culpepper grinned with a thought. The better the man, the more he enjoyed killing him. Besides, this time, Nate had an underlying personal cause for facing a man known to be good with weapons. He wanted to face the most lethal man possible and draw against him.

"Put my $2,500 advance money on the dresser, tell me who you want killed, and then get the hell out of my room."

"But, don't you want to hear all about this man?"

"Perhaps you didn't hear me. Put the money on the dresser, leave his name on that piece of paper and get out of my room. The contract is made. I'll do my part."

There it was. Nate Culpepper didn't care whom he faced. He was ugly, down to the bone mean and he didn't care who the target was. He would deliver his side of the contract, come hell or high water.

The well-dressed man left the room and Nate walked slowly, with legs slightly trembling in excitement to the dresser. He squinted hard at the name on the paper. He shook his head approvingly. He would face this man. He would face one of the most feared gunfighters in the West. He was to kill Cole Stockton, U.S. Marshal for the Lower Colorado.

"Cole Stockton," thought Culpepper. "Yes!" He would do it. Nate visualized: "Stockton will stand in front of me and look silently into my eyes. We will both know the other and we will each see the hell fire of the other's soul. He will know. He will draw with me, and then the fires of Hell will take the slowest. I know Stockton. I have seen his draw and I know that he will stand and take lead. It will be a gunfight worthy of my talent and worthy of my purpose."

CHAPTER TWO

A Dangerous Visitor

Just before the early dawn, the tall shadow stepped softly out of the darkened room of the Sumner Ranch house and made his way down the short hallway. He paused for a moment at the open door to let his eyes adjust to the dimness. He stepped into it and moved quietly toward the blanketed figure lying hugged to the pillow. He knelt down beside the bed.

Laura Lynne Sumner was deep in slumber when the soft hands touched her hair and brushed several loose strands from her face. She stirred quietly and then the soft lips were on her cheek and warm arms slid around her to hold her firmly for a long moment.

A hushed voice whispered, "Good morning. It's almost dawn, and I've got to ride into town. I'm planning on having breakfast with J.C. Kincaid. I should be back for supper."

A slight whimper responded from below Laura's bed.

"All right, Lady, come on, I'll let you out. I'll make coffee while you are doing your morning duty."

The shadow lightly brushed her cheeks once more, stood up and quietly moved through the ranch house to open the front door. A young dog playfully leaped out of the door to dash immediately to her favorite sniffing grounds.

Cole Stockton moved into the kitchen and started a fire in the cast iron stove. He filled the coffee pot with water and then ground a handful of coffee beans, dropping them into the pot.

A soft voice came from behind him. "So, trying to sneak out without a good luck hug, huh? Come here, Cole, hold me for a moment."

Cole moved into Laura Sumner's open arms and he felt the warmth of her soul. This tender embrace was the one central thought that he carried in the back of his mind while traveling the wilds in search of dangerous men.

Their embrace and kiss were long and warm.

"Now then, Cole Stockton, now you can go to town to talk your business. I just wanted you to know that you will be missed terribly."

"Laura, you sure know how to keep a man thinking about retiring some day. Maybe I will take off this badge today and just lay around this here ranch. I'm sure that you can find something for an unemployed old guy like me to do around here."

"There will be no handouts to out-and-out lazy men. My boys work for a living. Of course, if you want to be the ranch cook, I might have a place for you. Then again, I wonder just how long you would last before the wranglers strung you up because they had to eat beef jerky and cold biscuits all the time." Laura giggled playfully.

Cole laughed out loud. "You got a point there. No thanks, Laura. I'll keep the star, it's a lot safer."

The pair of them shared mugs of coffee together and then U.S. Marshal Cole Stockton made his way to the barn, saddled up Warrior, his dark chestnut with blazed face, mounted and rode out the gate toward town.

Laura watched her man ride off into the distance and suddenly a violent shudder ran through her body. She closed her eyes and a frightening vision flashed before her mind: *The blurred figure of a woman was struck hard across the mouth by a strong fist. The woman fell to earth unconscious, but then was quickly dragged to a horse, thrown across the saddle and lashed down. Another body lay bleeding beside a large wagon.*

The vision suddenly faded, as yet another vision took its place. *The shadows of two figures faced each other in a lonely street. Ruthless garble was exchanged. Hands flashed for revolvers, and in but a split second men, lay bleeding, near death on the hard ground.*

Laura sharply inhaled and held her breath. Her heart was pounding.

The vision appeared again. *One man shuddered before taking his last breath. His entire body was enveloped in flames—the eerie flames of Hell itself.*

She almost felt the dark shadows of the Devil's disciples gather up the ashes of the fallen and whisk them into a black bag, carrying them into the pit of eternal damnation.

The vision faded, and Laura Lynne Sumner stood there shivering in her night clothes.

* *

Nate Culpepper dismounted in front of the hotel in the small Colorado town near the passes to New Mexico. He slowly took in Main Street and mentally calculated the distance from building to building.

His dark eyes flashed brilliantly for this little town appeared made for a gunfight of his choosing. Yes, the measurements were precise. This would be the place. He drew his Winchester out of the scabbard, grabbed his saddlebags and then took one more slow sweep of the street with his eyes.

He looped the reins of his black mount over the hitching post before stepping wearily up onto the boardwalk of the hotel. He closed his eyes for a moment, then opened them.

Culpepper moved to the door of the hotel. He stepped inside and then slightly to the left to let his eyes become accustomed to the dimness of the interior. He made out the registration desk and walked a mite shakily toward it.

The unsuspecting desk clerk looked up directly into the coldest eyes he had ever seen in his life. He swallowed hard, and then asked, "What can I do for you, Sir?"

"I need a room. I need it for only two days and I'll pay in advance. Have your runner take my horse to the livery. Give it extra oats. I'll pay two days in advance for this service also. I want a room with a view of Main Street."

"Yes, Sir, that will be a dollar a night, fifty cents for the runner, and fifty cents for extra oats for two days. There is a bar right through them batwing doors, Sir, and just two doors down is an excellent café. A hot bath is available in the mornings—center of the floor. Is that all, Sir?"

Culpepper signed the register. He took the key from the hotel clerk, turned quickly and walked to the stairs. The clerk watched as the gunman momentarily made his way to the rail and then with a guarded glance slowly walked up the steps to the second floor.

The clerk examined the signature and exhaled with a rush. He now recognized the new guest. Those eyes! A cold start ran through the clerk's body and he shuddered with the intensity of it. This man, known for ruthlessness, was in this town to kill someone, of that, the clerk felt sure. There would be blood in the street within two days.

"I wonder who his intended victim is?" muttered John Kemp. "I think that I'd better send word to Sheriff Kincaid of this man's arrival."

* *

U.S. Marshal Cole Stockton sat with Sheriff J. C. Kincaid drinking coffee and spinning tall tales when the door to the jail opened and Johnny Williams, the hotel runner, stepped inside. Johnny looked quite wide-eyed and glanced around with wonder at the inside of the jail.

J.C. Kincaid spoke first. "Well, Johnny. How may I help you?"

"Oh, uh, Mr. Kemp, the hotel clerk sent me over to tell you that there's a man in town. He's staying at the hotel and said that he would only be here for a couple of days. He signed the register as *Nate Culpepper.*"

The sound of the name jolted J.C. Kincaid straight upright. Cole Stockton turned to face the young man. "<u>The</u> Nate Culpepper? Nate Culpepper, the Utah gunfighter?"

"Yessir," Johnny nodded rapidly. He is staying at the hotel. I took his horse to the livery for him."

J.C. Kincaid looked intently at Cole Stockton. "This reeks of another hiring to take you, Cole."

"Yes, J.C., it certainly does. Maybe I will just walk on down to the hotel and say howdy to our new visitor." Stockton rose from his wooden arm chair and moved toward the door of the jail.

"Cole. Wait a minute, I'll go with you. Let me get my shotgun."

"No, J.C. If Nate Culpepper wants me, then that shotgun ain't going to do worth a hill of beans. Besides, Culpepper doesn't work like that. He's always talked to his quarry before he called him out. I just want to worry him a bit by suddenly turning up in his face and checking him out. He won't try anything today."

"All right Cole, but if I hear gunfire, I'll run up there and blow his damned fool head off."

"Rest easy, J.C., I know what I am talking about. Culpepper likes to have an audience. His specialty is calling the man out and facing him in the middle of the street where all can see his handiwork."

Cole turned, stepped out of the jail, and strode purposely toward the hotel.

* *

Nate Culpepper lay quietly on his hotel room bed caressing the blue steel of his Colt Revolver.

He heard the jingle of spurs coming up the stairs, stopping for an instant, then moving down the hall toward his room. He listened intently. The spurs stopped just outside his door.

There came a soft knock, followed by a quiet voice, "Culpepper! Nate Culpepper! Open the door, this is Cole Stockton and I want to talk to you."

Culpepper bolted upright at the name. He slid off of the bed and fumbled his way to the center of the room. He slid his Colt into the holster, right hand hovering near it. He took a deep breath and answered. "Door's open. Come in and state your purpose."

The door swung open slowly to show a lone figure in the hallway. U.S. Marshal Cole Stockton stepped into the room where the two men faced each other for the first time.

Eyes met eyes and the heat of a thousand fires of soul-burning Hell passed between them before they spoke.

"So, what does the infamous Cole Stockton want with me, a simple traveling stranger to this town?"

"Don't give me that crap, Culpepper. I know you and I know you well. Just what the devil are you doing in this town?"

Culpepper grinned with an evil sneer.

"Why, Marshal Stockton, I just thought that I would ride on down here to Colorado and rid the world of the likes of you. I heard that you were the best. I aim to make you prove it–tomorrow at sun up. Meet me in the street. I will start from the hotel and we can meet in front of the Lady Luck Saloon. Best man wins and there'll be no begging for mercy. I will see you in Hell. What have you got to say about that, Mr. Marshal?"

Cole Stockton, eyes fixed, glared at the gunman. There was something wrong but Stockton couldn't put his finger on it. Culpepper was too anxious for this gunfight.

"All right, Culpepper. I'll meet you in the street at sunup." Stockton slowly backed toward the door, his eyes continuing to hold those of Nate Culpepper. Something in this hotel room was not right. It wasn't until Stockton reached the door and was turning away did he realize just what it was.

"I'll be dammed!" exclaimed Cole to himself as he exited the room and made his way down the stairs to the lobby.

Culpepper fumbled his way back to the bed and lay back. He closed his eyes as the sensation of death surged through his body. He shook uncontrollably for several minutes, before muttering his thoughts. "They said that you could feel the fires of Hell when you faced him. By God, it's true. For a moment there, I felt my soul burning."

Nate Culpepper looked intently at his hands. They were shaking. His palms were slick with sweat. Never in his life had he ever felt this way at meeting an adversary. Again he closed his eyes.

"Yes. It will be done."

CHAPTER THREE

The Lone Survivor

The Dakota-Colorado Butterfield Stagecoach swayed violently in the well-traveled, rut lined road from Bismarck, North Dakota into the ruggedly-wild Territory of Montana. Sammy Colter periodically shouted encouragement to his six-horse team as they plodded steadily along.

The coach slowed to a strained walk as it slowly made its way up a long grade. Once over the summit, Sammy Colter eased back on the reins and applied the foot brake. Now was the time to let the horses rest for fifteen minutes before moving along the boulder strewn road that led to the next curve, and down a long graded slope. A dense tree line stood magnificent and fresh along each side of the road.

A body could inhale the fresh scents of spruce, pine, wildflowers, and honeysuckle, even though every so often, these pleasant scents were mixed with a freshly laid odor of skunk. Deer and elk were frequently observed at a distance. Periodically, the coach passengers would hear the shrill shriek of an eagle as it majestically braked mid-air before streaking downward toward a distant creek or river.

Without warning, Sammy Colter jerked upright, slammed backward, and toppled over the side of the coach. The report of a rifle sounded almost instantaneously. The shotgun guard whipped up his Express shotgun and turned slowly to his right. When a second bullet split the air, George Altman hurled up and was literally thrown up and over the top of the coach, toppling to the ground. He never moved. Sammy Colter lay unconscious near the dead body of his friend and guard. A crimson stain spread along his shirt front.

Screaming and terrified passengers leaped from the coach to see what was happening. Johanna Stockton frantically made her way to lean over Sammy Colter.

"Sammy! My God! You've been shot! Speak to me, Sammy."

Six masked riders quickly swarmed the scene firing their revolvers into the air. One passenger, Ira Wooten, moved for his pocket pistol. He never knew what hit him. One second he held his pistol and a moment later, a heavy caliber bullet struck him down.

The other female passenger screamed as Wooten crumbled to the ground. A moment later, a bullet struck her in the back. She pitched forward with a loud moan dying on the hard ground.

The other two male passengers were shot at close range by the masked marauders, even as they raised their hands in surrender. The outlaws laughed as they riddled the two Easterners with multiple bullets.

Johanna turned to rise as two horsemen rounded the coach. She stood ramrod tall when one masked rider kicked out with his boot to smack her squarely in the face. Johanna tumbled back upon impact and slammed to the ground. Blood oozed from her mouth and nose. Her sight blurred as she slipped into semi-consciousness and her body numbed with pain.

All six riders dismounted and began rummaging through the coach. One climbed to the driver's box and threw down the Express box that contained the cash and gold. Another pointed his revolver at the lock and shot it open. His eyes gleamed with an evil, lusty look when he saw the neatly stacked bundles of greenbacks. He quickly counted the stacks and rows.

"Yah, Boys, didn't I tell you that this coach would be easy pickings? There must be over twenty thousand dollars here."

Just then, Johanna began to regain consciousness and moaned with pain.

One rider drew his revolver, cocking it as he turned toward Johanna, "No witnesses! Remember? We won't have anyone left to identify us."

He pointed the revolver at Johanna and was about to pull the trigger when another rider suddenly yelled at him. "Don't shoot her!"

"Why the hell not? She's just an old woman. Kind of pretty maybe, but she's lived her life. Let me put her out of her misery."

"You shoot that woman and I'll blow your brains out!" The young rider leveled his revolver straight at his partner and cocked it.

"What's the matter, Jamie? You getting soft? I thought we agreed. There will be NO witnesses."

"I didn't know that this woman would be on the stage when I agreed to that, Frank. You don't know who this woman is. I do! You kill that woman and there will be no safe place on the face of God's green earth for you. That woman is Johanna Stockton, the mother of Cole and Clay Stockton. Does that ring a bell with you, Frank?"

Nausea spread through Frank Sutton. He lowered his revolver and turned to the side of the road. He retched, knowing that he had almost sealed his own death, then turned to face Jamie Patterson, a shimmering residue of spittle streaming from his mouth.

"Damn! You mean that I almost killed Cole and Clay Stockton's mother?"

"That's exactly what I said, Frank."

"Are you sure about that?"

"As sure as I am sitting on this horse. I saw her with both of them back a couple months ago. They was a saying Yes Ma'am and No Ma'am to her. I caught some of the conversation and Clay Stockton called her Mother several times."

"Mother of God! If I had pulled that trigger, I'd be a walking dead man. Well, what do we do now?"

Jamie spoke up, "We will take her with us. She's bleeding, maybe hurt real bad, no thanks to Charlie. I think that if we treat her right, we might come out of this alive and well enough to spend that money. If we don't, we can be sure that U.S. Marshals Cole and Clay Stockton will be hot on our trail. They will not rest until all six of us are dead and buried. It seems best to head for Mexico and safety. We should keep the Stockton woman as our prisoner until we cross the border. Only then can we afford to release her. As long as she remains unharmed, we have a chance to spend that money. Are we in agreement?"

All of the outlaws wisely nodded their heads in agreement.

Johanna stirred again, attempting to get up. An intense flash of pain swept through her body before she lost consciousness once more.

Moments later, Johanna was only slightly aware that she was being lifted. More pain ravaged her body as she was draped over a hard saddle and tied securely. Minutes later, she felt the sway of the horse's gait as the six outlaws rode quickly down the slope and into the southward tree line. They headed south toward the passes of the Lower Colorado, New Mexico Territory, and the safety of the Mexican border.

Behind the renegades lay the deserted and rummaged Butterfield coach, the empty Express box, a dead shotgun guard, five dead passengers, and a severely wounded Sammy Colter hovering on the verge of death.

* *

Laura Sumner flitted earnestly around her kitchen preparing a fine supper of slow- roasted beef, potatoes, scallions, carrots, and smooth beef gravy. A large pan of fresh baked biscuits sat cooling on one side of the cast iron stove. A pot of freshly ground, dark coffee brewed on the back burner.

Laura heard the door open and shut somewhat harder than usual. She heard the jingle of Cole Stockton's spurs as he walked through the large front room, finally to stand at the kitchen door inhaling the delicious aromas.

When Laura looked into his eyes, she saw a troubled look. "What is it, Cole?"

"I've been called out. I have to face a man tomorrow at sunup."

"Oh, Cole! Not again! Who is it? Is he good? Can you take him?"

"Laura, this time it's Nate Culpepper."

"God, Cole. I have read of him. He's known to be extremely fast. The rumor is he's vicious." Laura shuddered at the thought of Cole facing this evil man.

"Yes, Laura, he is a no-good. He was acquitted for his last encounter. The other man drew first."

"And you, Cole, just what are you going to do?"

"I already told you, Laura. I am going to face him in the morning. Only--only, I just don't know yet."

"What is it, Cole? What is on your mind? Is there something you aren't telling me?"

"Yes, Laura. You see, I visited Culpepper this afternoon in his hotel room."

"You did what?"

"I visited Culpepper in his hotel room. The shades were drawn making the room quite dim. I watched his eyes, Laura, and there was no fire to them, yet he called me out. It is like he wants to die. As a matter of fact, Laura, I think that he is going blind. Yes, I think that he is going blind, and he knows that if anyone finds out about it, there will be so many scavengers looking for a reputation on his back that he will be shot down by mere amateurs."

Cole continued, "I think that he wants me to kill him so he can go out in his own blaze of glory—bested by someone faster and better than he, or he wants to take someone as equally good with him. That, Laura, just turns my stomach. Just think about it, a man who gives no mercy is now pleading for a type of mercy killing himself. I will have to think on it some. Is that coffee ready? I could sure use a cup right now."

Laura moved into Cole's arms to feel his arms slide around her and hold her firmly to him. She knew what he was thinking. That there would be justice was beyond question. She snuggled more firmly to him.

* *

The afternoon passed quietly and the six stagecoach horses were hungry, weary, and yearning to lie down and roll amongst tall grasses. Still, no one moved. The horses fidgeted in their traces.

A low moan came from Sammy Colter only a moment before his eyes rolled open. Near dusk, the veteran driver swallowed hard as the nausea passed. He felt the crust of dried blood on his face. He glanced at the red stain on his shirt and felt the pain of the molten lead inside his gut.

For a long moment, his eyes refused to focus. Pulling himself up on one elbow he saw the senseless carnage that the outlaws left behind. One thought raced through his mind causing a scream as loud as his lungs could muster, "Johanna!"

Sammy Colter carefully looked around the coach and he could account for all of the dead but one—Johanna. "Oh my God, they've taken Johanna! I've got to do something. I've got to get up and do something."

Pain shot through his body, but his mind was kind, delivering him into the world of unconsciousness.

* *

The night broke softly over the mountain top and shed complete darkness on the world. A small campfire flickered, flames eagerly licking at the dry wood that was fed into it periodically.

Five men gathered near the fire, gleaning its warmth while eating a supper of stew, beans, and biscuits. One man sat a short distance from the fire beside the feverish body of Johanna Stockton. He spoke in a soothing voice to her while he methodically applied wet cloths from the nearby stream to her bruised and swollen face.

"Just lay still, Ma'am. No harm will come to you. I want to help you. I am truly sorry that you were hurt."

Johanna mumbled through the pain of her body. "You robbed and killed those people on the coach. They didn't do any harm to you. You just up and killed them."

The young man swallowed hard. He saw the pain and sorrow in Johanna's eyes and a deep guilt swept over him. After a pause to search for words, he replied, "Yes, Ma'am. They are all dead except for you. You are our prisoner and you will be released when we cross the border into Mexico. Please, for your own safety, just do as you are told, when you are told, and you will be spared."

Johanna Stockton's heart sank as she realized the gravity of the young man's words. She looked up into his eyes, "You know who I am, young man, don't you?"

"Yes. I know that you are the mother of Cole Stockton and Clay Stockton."

"Then, you know they are coming to find me."

"Yes. I know that also."

"Do you also know what they will do when they find me with you?"

The young man was quite nervous and Johanna saw his hands tremble at her words.

"They are going to kill all of you who put up a fight. Those that drop their guns will be arrested and charged with robbery, murder, and kidnapping their mother. What will you do, young man, when you are looking down the bore of their guns knowing you are about to die?"

"Shut up. Please, just shut up. Don't say anything more."

"You are scared, aren't you? It shows on your face and in your trembling hands."

"Yes, I am damned scared. I don't want to die. I stopped them from killing you when I suddenly realized who you are. I know that your sons will track us to the ends of the earth if any harm comes to you. I won't let any more harm come to you. I will protect you with my life until we cross the border."

"Son, you've got that all wrong because no border in the world is going to stop those two. You are going to have to face them, and be reckoned with. What is your name, son?"

"Jamie. Jamie Patterson."

"Well, Jamie. Think about it. You will have to face two men with great knowledge of weapons, two men with determination. Two men who would rather die than give up. Can you do that? I have seen both of them wounded and still they stood on their feet shooting the men that had broken the law. Is that what you want?"

"Oh, no! I just want to get away from all of this and just live my life."

"You can't run away from it, Jamie. It will haunt you all of your life. Help me return to my sons Help me go back and I will speak for you."

17

"Ma'am, I can't do that. I have sworn to these men. These men are my friends and I am with them to the last. You know how it is."

"Yes, Jamie, I suppose that I do. But, are these men really your friends? Well, in a few days, it won't matter anymore. All six of you will be dead and buried."

CHAPTER FOUR

Hour of the Gunfighter

Dawn broke over the mountain top as the darkness of the night was replaced with both sunshine and gray shadows. Nate Culpepper rose from his hotel bed. He meticulously washed, shaved, and dressed in his best suit like he was going to a funeral. Lastly he picked up his gun belt and strapped it on, settling it to his most comfortable position. He tested his draw, letting his arms hang loosely with his wrists barely touching the butts of the twin Colts. He felt satisfied.

Culpepper moved to the door of his room, opened it and stepped carefully down the hallway to the stairs. He slowly descended to the lobby of the hotel, using the hand rail for balance. He walked on slightly unsteady feet to the door. He paused for a moment then took a deep breath. A single thought, once again, blazed across his mind, "Well, this is the day. I am facing a man whom I consider my equal. Perhaps both of us will die today, but the task must be completed."

Nate pushed open the heavy door and moved out into the street. He paused for a moment to inhale the fresh mountain air. Stepping off the boardwalk, he moved to stand in the exact center of the dusty street before turning toward the far end of town.

He grinned with an evil smile as he saw the tall, slender figure move to the center of the street a hundred yards from him. The two men began the walk of death toward one another.

Nate silently appraised Cole Stockton walking toward him. His adversary was wearing only one revolver and his hand was never too far from the butt of that deadly Colt. The man walked slowly and naturally. There seemed to be no fear in the man's stature.

Culpepper silently said a prayer that he couldn't see Cole Stockton's eyes. It was said by many that to look into Stockton's eyes was to look into the very depths of Hell itself and that one could feel the searing, burning fires of eternal damnation.

The two men stopped at thirty yards apart to stand and appraise each other. It was Culpepper that spoke first, "Glad to see that you could make it, Stockton. Are you prepared to die? I am!"

"There will be no dying today, Culpepper! I know that you are going blind and I refuse to draw against you, let alone kill you for your own gratification. You will have to live with your situation and take life as it comes."

"I'll be dammed if I will. I will force you to draw. If you don't, I'll shoot you dead."

"I think not, Culpepper. You can't see well enough to aim for me—not even at thirty yards which was once your favorite distance."

"Damn you, Stockton!"

Culpepper flashed for his twin revolvers. The draw was magnificently fast and within a split second both weapons blossomed with bright orange flame.

Culpepper's mouth opened wide in surprise when he heard both bullets smack into the building at the far end of the street.

"See, Culpepper? I told you that you couldn't aim straight."

"Just keep talking, you SOB. I'll pin you down, and then we'll see who can't shoot straight."

A long silence followed as Culpepper made out the blurry figure step into the deep shadows of the nearest buildings. Stockton seemed to disappear. Culpepper shouted in frustration, "Come on out and face me you coward. Shoot at me. Come on, try and kill me!"

Still silence.

Culpepper started forward, catching himself before he stumbled in the dusty street. He had gone but ten feet when he heard the unmistakable "click" of metal sliding against metal. It was the cocking of a revolver behind him. A moment later, he felt the touch of cold steel against the back of his neck.

Culpepper stopped in his tracks and inhaled sharply. He shook with dire fear. Cole Stockton had circumvented him in the shadows and come silently up behind him to place his Colt right up against the back of his neck and cocked it.

Stockton's stealthy action unnerved the gunfighter sending waves of terror through his body. His entire body shook like the very Devil himself was standing behind him.

"Drop your guns, Culpepper. The show is over."

Nate Culpepper lowered his face toward the ground and opened his hands. Both Colts dropped onto the street with a thud. His face grimaced as the agony of defeat spread through his mind and body.

"I wanted to die by a hand better than mine. At the last moment, I just couldn't do it. I,m a coward."

"No, Nate. You want to live. No man really wants to die. You are a brave man to even face me this morning. Now, I'll take your guns. You go back to your hotel room and think about leaving the West. Go someplace where young men with guns don't hunt down a man with a reputation. Go somewhere where you can do some good for the world. Maybe, go East and write some books on your experiences. Tell readers that would seek out the way of the gun that it just ain't worth it."

"You know, don't you, Stockton? I have lived with the silence and the remembrances of many deaths for so long now. I can still see their faces, both young and old. They haunt me, Cole Stockton, and now maybe, I can get free of their presence."

"Be on the noon stage toward the East, Nate. Don't ever think about coming back."

"I'll be on it. Before I go, though, there is a matter of just why I am here. Just thought you'd like to know. I was paid five thousand dollars to kill you. Track down three men. Their names are Orin Freemire, Jeff Oates, and last but not least, Frederick Canton. Yes, the old cattle baron himself wants you out of the way for some reason. We are even now."

"Thanks, Nate. Just be on that stagecoach."

Nate Culpepper, once known as the fastest man in Utah and parts around, made his way slowly and without fanfare to the hotel and disappeared.

Cole Stockton waited a long moment before reaching down to pick up the twin Colt Revolvers that had belonged to one of the most deadly men in the West. He shoved them down into his belt.

Without warning, a shot rang out from the hotel.

Cole bolted to the boardwalk, and rushed through the doors. He shot a questioning glance at John Kemp who stammered and pointed up the stairs.

Stockton bounded up the stairs and down the hallway. He found Culpepper's door cracked and without hesitation kicked it wide open.

The Marshal entered the room with drawn Colt, but quickly holstered it. Nate Culpepper lay on the floor in the center of the room, a pool of blood flowing from around his head. A small .41 caliber pistol lay beside his lifeless hand. Nate Culpepper had taken his own life rather than face a life of blindness.

* *

Sammy Colter roused briefly in the cool night. He opened his eyes and made an attempt to focus on what appeared to be millions of brilliantly lit stars. When he tried to move, sharp pain shot through his body. He shivered and once again passed out.

Toward dawn Colter felt the touch of leathery hands on his face as fingers probed near his wound. He winced sharply and opened his eyes only to stare into the somber face of an Indian.

Sammy's eyes went wide as the Indian reached to his belt and withdrew a long sharp knife. He screamed loudly with fear for his life.

"Shut up, old man. Indians might hear you and then we will both be in heap big trouble," barked the knife wielding Indian.

"Just who the devil are you?"

"They call me Spotted Hawk. I scout for Yankee blue coats at Fort Lyon. You lay still now, no talk. I look at wound."

Sammy Colter took several deep breaths of relief as Spotted Hawk slid the knife to his shirt front and with one quick movement neatly sliced his entire front open to reveal the purple hole of a bullet wound surrounded with swollen red flesh.

"Lucky for you Spotted Hawk come. I see many times. Many men die from same wound. You one lucky son-of-a-gun. I fix for you. You be strong like great bear from the North in two days. Maybe even like great bull buffalo."

"But--but, the bullet has come out."

"Yes, old one. No worry. Spotted Hawk take bullet out. You rest easy for now. I fix strong medicine. You sleep much. Spotted Hawk make strong medicine and take out bullet. You see."

"Well, I ain't never seen the likes."

"What mean?"

"Aw shut up and get to work Injun."

"Be good old man. Maybe I scalp you before you wake up." A smile came with this instruction. Spotted Hawk liked Sammy already.

Without another word, Sammy Colter shut his mouth and didn't move. He closed his eyes and one figure loomed close in his mind– Johanna. Sammy breathed deeply and thought of the one woman that kindled the fires of his very heart and soul. He prayed for her safety.

The next thing he knew, Spotted Hawk held a strange pouch of fine powder in one hand and a canteen of water in the other.

"Open big mouth, old man. This strong medicine. Make you sleep much. Good! Now drink big."

Sammy followed the instruction. In a moment he felt very drowsy and calm. The pain left his body, his eyes dilated. His last memory was floating on the easy waters of the Mississippi when he was a boy. He called out, "Yes, Ma'am. I'm coming, Mother".

Sammy drifted off into the world of deep dreams and revisited his youth.

Spotted Hawk watched the wounded stage driver as he drifted into an unconscious state. He nodded his approval. His medicine was strong and he could save this grizzled old man.

The wily Indian reached for his hunting knife which he had set in the hot coals of a small fire. He blew on it softly. Spotted Hawk skillfully began the procedure to remove the chunk of lead from Colter's body.

After a long hour of tedious probing and precise cutting, Spotted Hawk held the bullet up and looked at it. The bullet was intact. It had not split nor blossomed. He looked down on the old stage driver.

"You lucky Spotted Hawk come. I take bullet. Now you sleep. You need rest. Spotted Hawk take care of you."

Sammy Colter stirred a bit in his deep stupor and called out, "Johanna. They've taken Johanna!"

Spotted Hawk quickly bent to Sammy and had him repeat the words.

Spotted Hawk understood what Sammy said.

"Bad men take my friend. I must get message to great warrior, Marshal Stock-ton. Bad men take his mother."

While Sammy slept, Spotted Hawk buried the dead from the stagecoach, and in the morning, the Army scout took the coach stock along with Sammy Colter and rode toward the house of the singing wire. Perhaps, he thought, he could get the station master to send a message to U.S. Marshal Cole Stockton.

CHAPTER FIVE

Colorado Territory

Johanna and her six abductors woke to an early Montana frost that chilled them to the bone. Wood was hastily placed on the simmering coals of the night's fire. Hungry flames licked at the wood as they devoured the length.

A glowing warmth spread slowly over the camp.

Jamie Patterson stood beside Johanna holding his hand out to her.

"Come, Mrs. Stockton. You are shivering. Come to the fire to be warmed."

Johanna allowed herself to be brought upright and together they walked up close to the blazing fire. Johanna trembled for a long moment, then knelt down near enough to hold her icy cold hands to the warmth of the flames.

One of the men placed a coffee pot on a large flat rock into the fire. Within fifteen minutes the smell of freshly brewed coffee drifted aimlessly on the early morning air. All present inhaled its aroma and produced their tin cups in anticipation of their share of its stimulating warmth.

One of the men announced to the others, "Well, this being September, it looks like they are in for one hard winter up here in Montana. When do you reckon that we will hit the passes of Colorado into New Mexico?"

Another spoke up, "I figure that we will be there in just about a week if we keep traveling fast and hard and ain't got nothing to slow us down." When he looked menacingly toward Johanna, she shook at his evil stare.

Jamie Patterson responded to Simon Blakely with set determination, "You never mind your ugly thoughts, Simon. The woman will ride with me and if you think that we are slowing you down, well, just ride on ahead and be gone with you."

Blakely replied, "I want my share before I go."

Jamie reminded the him, "We all agreed that the money will be divided amongst those of us that reach the safety of Mexico, and not until then. You leave the group, you lose your share."

"All right then, but if that woman holds us back, I'll do the deed myself and then we will be free to travel fast."

"You will have to kill me first, Simon," challenged Jamie.

"That won't be no problem—sonny. Just stand up and we'll do it now."

Jamie started to rise but was stopped by a sharp word from Zed Thomas.

"Stop it, damn you two. There will be no gunplay between us. If them Marshals catch up to us, we will need every gun, and there will be gunplay enough for all. Set yourselves down and shut up. Jamie, the woman is yours to take care off. See that you do it."

"I will, Zed. Tell that SOB to back off."

Simon glared at Jamie. One day soon he was going to kill both Johanna and that young Jamie. It would be very soon, just about the time that they cleared the passes into New Mexico. He would enjoy it immensely, because he hadn't liked the kid since the day that he met him. Two bullets and there would be one less to split the stage loot with. That thought brought on another thought—what if, just what if, he Simon were the only one to cross into Mexico. He would have the entire take to himself. A man could live a long, long time in Mexico with money like that and the more he thought about it, the more he liked it.

* *

Spotted Hawk rode slowly into the small community with its stagecoach way station, trading post, and telegraph office. Sammy Colter lay wrapped in bandages on the travois behind one of the coach team horses.

Several Indian women and children sat leisurely on the porch to the trading post. There were a few rough looking frontier men passing the time as well. The smell of fresh hides, unwashed bodies, and stale beer permeated the boardwalk.

Spotted Hawk raised his hand to a couple of the wild-looking men dressed in buckskin clothing with long greasy hair. They nodded back in recognition, then moved forward to see what manner of man or beast was riding the makeshift stretcher dragged behind the horse.

Questions from the men peppered Spotted Hawk before he could dismount. "What you done got there, Spotted Hawk? Damn, looks like a wounded white man. Where did you find him, Spotted Hawk? Did you go back on the warpath? How come he ain't scalped like the rest of them that you brung in?"

Sammy Colter's eyes sprung open and went wide.

As the spectators gathered around Sammy, one spoke to reassure him. "Aw take it easy, Old Timer, we is just funning. Old Spotted Hawk there was some kind of warrior chief in his younger day. Good thing that he is scouting for the Army now, I'd hate to have him tracking me down for the kill. He's a crafty old buzzard."

Spotted Hawk smiled as he shook his head approvingly. He knew that these scouts had an awesome respect for his many talents. That was why they were good friends.

"Got to send two wires and FAST!" babbled out Sammy Colter. "The southbound coach has been robbed and all killed except for me and a woman. Them murderous SOB's took the woman with them. They's headed for Mexico. The woman that they took is a good friend of mine and not only that—she is the mother of U.S. Marshals Cole and Clay Stockton. Help me write out them there wires and get them sent."

One old scout spoke up, "God Almighty, you don't say. By gum, them boys will never live to see Mexico. I've heard of both of them

Stockton boys and by all accounts they's faster than greased lightning and twice as deadly as a coiled rattler. I heard once that Cole Stockton took lead from three men and still killed them boys and three others in a close-in saloon gunfight. I heard too that Clay Stockton took two rifle bullets at close range and before he hit the ground had nailed both of them gunmen straight in the heart. Man, that was some shooting. Both of them boys are dammed hard to kill—many has tried, and they are all dead and buried. I shore wouldn't want to be in them kidnappers' boots when the Stockton boys catch up to them."

Another scout chipped in his thoughts, "Nor would anyone in their right mind. There is no safe place on God's green earth when them two get their dander up."

* *

Clay Stockton read the brief telegram twice before he turned to his Deputy.

"Sandy! Come here. I am riding out within the hour. The southbound coach has been robbed and all killed except for Sammy Colter and Ma. The men responsible have taken Ma prisoner and I am riding after them. Wire on ahead to all lawmen and coach stations along the route from Montana to the Lower Colorado. I want to do a Pony Express style run. I want a fresh horse saddled and ready, and a cup of hot black coffee waiting on me when I get to those stations."

Clay Stockton dashed out the door to the livery to saddle up and Deputy Sandy Merrick hurried to the telegraph office.

Fifteen minutes later Clay Stockton galloped out of Bismarck, North Dakota like the very Devil was on his heels. He was headed for Montana and then through Wyoming to the Wilds of the Lower Colorado.

* *

Miles away, Cole Stockton and Laura Sumner sat casually sipping coffee with Sheriff J.C. Kincaid at the Miller's Station jail.

"J.C., this has got to be the BEST coffee that you have ever made," remarked Laura.

"Yah, I finally got the hint. Cole told me how to make it. Now, I just grind up a whole lot of beans and make it just as strong as I want."

J.C. Kincaid gave a questioningly look toward Cole Stockton and saw that silly grin spread slowly over his face. He was about to say something when the door to the jail flew open. There stood Jimmy, the telegraph runner, out of breath, waving a telegram.

"Hey there, Jimmy. Stop! You need to take a deep breath. What is it that has got you up in a tither?"

"I got a mighty urgent wire for Marshal Stockton. I saw Warrior and Mickey out front and I just knew that he would be here. Marshal Stockton—your Ma has been taken by coach robbers and murderers. They killed everyone on the southbound coach except for your Ma and the driver. Word has it that they are headed toward the passes for Mexico." Jimmy spurted the entire message before taking a breath, now he gasped for air.

Cole took the telegram from Jimmy and read it twice before passing it to Laura Sumner. Laura read it and then looked deep into Cole Stockton's eyes. The glimmer of death and destruction shined brightly and she could feel the intensity of his rising anger.

She rose and placed her hand on Cole's shoulder. "What do you want me and the boys to do Cole? We will help in any way possible."

"I'd like for you and your wranglers to watch the wilds very carefully. If any sign of about six men and a woman should show itself, I want to be the first to know. Then he addressed everyone in the jail office. In the meantime, Clay is riding hell bent for leather to join up with me. I want to put all the lookouts possible along the passes. Don't any of you try to stop them nor interfere. Clay and I will handle this situation. Do I make myself clear?" Everyone nodded agreement.

Laura trembled slightly. She caught the unmistakable aura of death in Cole's voice and she swallowed hard. They had taken Johanna. They had taken Cole and Clay Stockton's mother and now there would be hell to pay.

* *

The marauding six, along with their hostage Johanna in tow, rode the tree lines and gullies of the Montana Territory and Wyoming in a conscious effort to pass unseen through the untamed sparsely populated countryside. Several days later, the distant peaks of the snow-capped Colorado Rocky Mountains loomed in the near distance. They stopped momentarily to stretch their legs and rest the horses.

"Well, Boys," announced one, "that there is the wilds of Colorado. Once we get into those thick forests of aspen, pine, and spruce there is not a man alive that can track us. We will travel unseen until we reach the passes into New Mexico Territory. After that, there is wide open spaces, sagebrush, and cacti for miles and miles. Then comes ole Mexico and the good life."

Johanna's thoughts produced a smile as she looked up at the snowy peaks of the distant mountains. They were almost in Colorado now and within a few days travel would be within shouting distance of the Sumner Ranch. She closed her eyes and thought of her eldest son. She envisioned Laura Sumner's ranch, and momentarily Laura's vision loomed close in her mind. She trembled slightly, and then hugged herself.

Jamie looked over to Johanna and actually saw the shiver surge through her body. Her eyes grew bright with hope.

Without warning, the young man was overcome with unexplained emotion. A rush of panic moved through his body and he found himself having to grab hold of his saddle horn in order to stay mounted.

Within a few moments the fear subsided and he breathed a long hard sigh of relief. He looked again at Johanna. There seemed to be an aura of light all around her.

Jamie Patterson had never experienced something this strong before. It was as though the light of an angel came from the heavens above. He swallowed hard and touched the butt of his revolver. It felt cold and hard to his touch. Always before, it had seemed warm and close to his being.

Jamie closed his eyes for a long moment. Recollections of his early life formed before his mind. He smiled. And then, an evil figure swept before his mind's eye, causing Jamie Patterson to feel an immediate sensation of anguish as his soul was enveloped in the fires of Hell. At that very moment, Jamie Patterson felt that he would never reach Mexico. He believed that he would die on the trail, and perhaps be buried in some lonely unmarked grave. He glanced again at Johanna and found that she was looking toward him. She reached out and gently touched his hand and a flow of warmth surged through him.

Johanna whispered to Jamie, "Give me your revolver and turn your back."

Jamie closed his eyes for a moment. "No, Mrs. Stockton. I can't do that. Don't worry, I will take care of you."

Johanna nodded without a word. She knew that he couldn't, but it was worth a try. The two of them nudged their mounts forward to catch up with the others.

* *

Clay Stockton rode a sweat-frothed horse into each coach station along the road to the Colorado Territory. When darkness made it impossible to see trails with dangers lurking abundantly, Clay reluctantly halted at the last swing station before Colorado. He dismounted wearily from the exhausted dun and led it to the stable. He struggled to stand upright but, with angry determination, forced himself to rub down the animal, and to feed and water it. He closed his eyes, thinking of his mother. A soft light crossed his mind and he knew that Johanna was safe for the time being.

Exhausted, Clay knew that he must sleep. He stumbled into the coach swing station and devoured two plates of beef and beans, drank a couple of cups of dark coffee, and ate three slices of berry pie. Next, he stumbled to a bunk, closed his eyes, and fell immediately into deep slumber.

* *

In the meantime, Cole Stockton sat huddled in front of his small camp fire. His face was grim and he was deep in thought.

He had purposely chosen this site. From this high vantage point, he could see the distant glow of various towns and ranches for miles around. He knew instinctively which were towns and which were ranches or farms. He also recognized small flickers as campfires.

Cole reached into his saddle bags to withdraw a couple of pieces of beef jerky. He ripped off a piece with his teeth and began to chew slowly, savoring the juices. He enjoyed the taste and it helped him ponder his plan. He went over the events of the coach murders, robbery, and kidnapping.

These were no ordinary thieves. These men were evil men. They wanted no witnesses to their deed and all of it indicated a plan from the start. Cole thought long and hard. What brand of men were these that would kill innocent people who chose to travel this specific coach? He finally came to his decision: this group must have some hard scavengers mixed with perhaps some younger rowdies that looked for fame and fortune.

Perhaps, he thought, that there might be a falling out amongst them. Why had Johanna been taken? Why was she not killed like all the rest? No. There must be at least one man amongst them that was taken with her. Could it be an older scoundrel or was it a much younger man that suddenly had thoughts of his own mother?

The chill of an early frost penetrated Cole Stockton's thoughts and he pulled his bedroll closer around him. He lay back and withdrawing his revolver placed it close to hand under the bedding.

Cole closed his eyes and saw his mother. A warm feeling enveloped him and he too knew that she was safe for the moment. His thoughts of Johanna faded, and were replaced by another. He envisioned Laura

Sumner. She lay asleep in her bed and the eerie light of a blood red moon filtered over her face.

Cole shivered as an all-consuming, soul-burning fire burned brightly within the recesses of his mind.

He knew exactly what he had to do. Cole Stockton's fingers trembled as he reached to the Silver Star on his vest. He touched it and it felt cold. He fumbled as he unpinned Cole the star of authority and slipped it to his inside vest pocket. His eyes turned cold, hard and uncaring as his fingers reached up and touched the butt of his Colt Revolver.

CHAPTER SIX

Mean to the Bone

Clay Stockton awoke to the aroma of fresh coffee, biscuits, bacon, and fried potatoes. He inhaled deeply. He couldn't remember when he had eaten last, although it had been just before he climbed exhausted into the bed that he now occupied.

He slowly sat up and wearily forced his legs to slide to the floor. He took a deep breath, then exhaled. He felt tired, but he must go on. He must catch up with the men who killed five passengers, left Sammy Colter for dead and took his mother captive.

Clay forced himself into his boots. He stood, stretched his lanky frame, then grabbed his gun belt. He slapped it around his slim waist, then reached down under the pillow and withdrew the well-cared for Colt. He looked at it for a long moment. Silently, and without emotion, Clay Stockton reached up to his vest front and unpinned the Silver Star of authority that kept him within the bounds of the law. He swallowed hard, then placed the star into his rumpled jacket pocket. He took another deep breath. "This manner of men needs not see this star. My motive is personal and as I live and breathe, if one hair on her head has been wronged, I will kill the men responsible. So help me."

Clay Stockton dragged his weary body into the main room of the coach station. The welcome sight of platters of fried eggs, bacon, beef steak, biscuits, jam, and pots of dark black coffee greeted him.

He directed the station master to have a horse saddled and ready within half an hour, before grabbing up a chair to sit down and fill a plate with a hearty breakfast.

34

Clay was about to finish his breakfast when the front door to the station swung wide and two figures appeared against the early light of dawn. Clay looked up and grinned. Spotted Hawk and Sammy Colter came near him. Both nodded their greetings, sat down across the table from him and filled plates with food.

Sammy looked over Clay Stockton from head to foot, "Something is missing, Clay. Where is your star?"

"I don't need the star for this," was Clay's somber reply.

The old coach driver was about to say something else, but it was Spotted Hawk that spoke first, "You mighty Warrior, Mar-shall Clay. I know of your many brave deeds. You have killed many enemies in battle. You have counted many coups. You like ancient warrior of my people. You protect those who cannot defend themselves. You are mighty in my eyes. I know many you have helped. They speak to me of much respect. Even my people speak of the justice you have brought to this land—justice for all people. It is not right that you take off sacred symbol. You must think on this."

Spotted Hawk continued, "If one man, even mighty warrior, can kill enemies and not be judged, then why does the white man judge the red man for the same thing? I do not understand this. Does it suit the white man to kill an enemy whenever he feels it is right, and not to be judged for this? Speak to me of this. Help me to understand this. Is not the sacred symbol of the great sky a sign to all those who see it, that this man who wears this symbol as a mighty warrior, should be treated with much respect? Is it not true that the warrior who wears such symbol have much honor. I am sorry. I do not know why you take off sacred symbol of the night skies. It means much to my people. It means that there is one who can be trusted to make everything fair to all people."

Clay Stockton looked deep into the eyes of Spotted Hawk.

"This is different. This is my mother that those men have taken."

"Would it be any different if it were a young woman of the Southern Cheyenne that was taken? I think so. I have seen this from other men who have worn the Sacred star and have used it for their own good. Is this, Mar-shall Clay, what you want?"

Clay Stockton thought long and hard. He slowly nodded his head and reached into his coat pocket. He fingered the Silver Star of United States Marshal and then re-pinned it to his shirt front.

"Makes a good target, don't it?"

Sammy Colter let out a sigh and spoke his mind, "My sentiments exactly, Clay. But, you can't just take off the badge when you want to. Besides, when it comes right down to it, I don't think that you could do it. I don't think that you could kill a man just because you took your badge off. I know you, Clay Stockton. You are too much like Cole. I have seen Cole take that star off and on, and just between you and me, he always puts it back on before he shoots. There is some kind of honor that just won't let him kill for the sheer hell of it. I, too, Clay, see it in your eyes. You are a man of the West. You are gifted in your skills."

Sammy continued, "Sometimes I wish that I had the gift too, but right now, between you and Cole, you are all we got to bring these men to justice. If they fight, you will shoot them. That's understood. But, iffen you shoot them boys down in anger, you will never live it down. Bring back them that drop their guns. Talk to Cole about it, too. Damn! Iffen I could, I would ride with you, but I have this one arm in a sling."

"Sammy, can you shoot?" asked Clay.

"Why, yes, I can, with my left hand. What's that got to do with it?"

"Sammy, raise your left hand. Spotted Hawk, your right hand and swear after me. I do solemnly swear to uphold the laws of the United States and all its territories, so help me God."

Spotted Hawk raised his right hand as did Sammy Colter his left. "What mean God?"

"The Great Spirit."

"O.K., I do. We track them bad men down and then, we be like ancient warrior. We ride straight into their camp and shoot them."

"That's exactly what I had in mind, Spotted Hawk."

"Me, too," mumbled Sammy.

"Well then, you two are sworn Deputy United States Marshals. Are you finished with yore breakfast? Let's ride. We need to reach Cole before he runs across them guys by himself. There is no telling what he would do."

* *

Zed Thomas led his band of murdering outlaws and their captive toward the passes of the Lower Colorado and northern New Mexico. He increasingly smiled the closer they came to the passes into New Mexico. Finally, Thomas pulled up short and looked hard into the distance. "Well, boys. There she is. See that dip in the landscape over yonder. There is the beginning of the passes. We should be there by noon tomorrow."

Johanna Stockton held a smile in her heart. She also had been watching the landscape very carefully. She recognized this very place where she now sat her mount. She had traveled over it with her son and his special friend Laura Sumner not two months past.

Johanna calculated that they were within a day's ride of the Sumner Ranch. That meant that she was within a day's ride of all of the help that she could ever want. She closed her eyes and thought of her eldest son.

A spark of hope, passed through her body. Yes, she knew that Cole Stockton was on the trail somewhere ahead. She also knew that he was waiting for them. Tears filled her eyes.

Jamie Patterson rode up alongside of her and noticed the blush of her cheeks and tears running down them. "Are you crying Mrs. Stockton? Is there something I can do?"

"No, Jamie. There is nothing you can do right now. Perhaps we can talk later tonight."

"Sure thing, Mrs. Stockton. We'll talk after supper."

The pair rode in silence together the remainder of the day. In the evening when their meager supper of beans, biscuits, and coffee was finished, Johanna sat back from the glow of the fire and held thoughts to herself.

Jamie Patterson approached the once injured woman and sat down beside her with one last cup of dark brew. He spoke in a tone the others could not hear. "I've been thinking, Mrs. Stockton. I've been thinking a lot since a few days ago when you asked me to turn my back and let you run. I can't turn my back and let you go--but, I can run with you. How far do you think we can get before they catch up to us. I mean, we can't hold them boys off for long. We need a safe place to run to and it can't be very far away."

"Jamie. When the time is right, I will let you know. We both must gallop off at the same time and ride like the very Devil himself is on our tail. I want a revolver also. Together we can hold them for a while. I don't know if you realize it or not, but all of you are treading in very dangerous territory right now. My son Cole will be on us before we reach those passes—of that I am sure. We must break away from these men and, for your safety, be together when Cole finds us."

Near sundown the group paused to look once more at the distant passes in anticipation of riding through them near noon the next day. One of the outlaws looked to the rear and swallowed hard. He shouted to the others, "Look there, in the sky behind us. Smoke, a smoke signal by gum. That's an Injun smoke signal iffen I ever saw one, and it's only about five miles away. Look for an answering signal somewhere."

Before much time passed there was smoke rising into the southern sky ahead. Zed and his men shot glances toward one another without a word.

Simon spoke up, "What you all so nervous about? We got the woman, ain't we? If that's Injuns, or the law, we can whop them. We'll trade her life for ours and be off to Mexico."

Zed nodded. He felt his men were still with him. "All right, let's get off this trail and make camp up in them pines. Keep the fire low so it don't give sign of us. Everyone stays awake tonight. We've got to be very careful from here on out."

The perpetrators kept eyes and ears open to various sounds and movements throughout the long night. Only the long, low howl of wolves in the distance along with the occasional hoot of an owl were distinguishable during their watch.

Near dawn as the outlaws were saddling up, preparing to move toward the nearest pass, the shrill sound of a Cheyenne war whistle split the din of the morning. It was followed by the war scream of a

Cheyenne warrior. Without warning, a painted warrior rode through the camp firing his rifle.

Hot lead blazed through the camp, smacked trees and camp fire, showering the ground with hot ashes. A few of the outlaws found themselves ducking quick to avoid being burned with the hot ash. As quickly as it began, it was over. Silence. A dead silence. The wild Indian had vanished into the thick stands of pine up slope of them.

Several minutes passed. Then, suddenly, six quick cracks of a revolver burst through the still air causing all in camp to dive into the dirt and take cover.

Johanna lay flat on the ground. Jamie crawled to lie next to her.

"Well, young man, I think that the time is here. Give me a revolver and let's get the hell out of here."

Jamie turned to thrust a revolver at Johanna. She smiled as she felt the smooth grip in her hand.

Jamie and Johanna stood up and quickly ran to the horses. Incredibly, no bullets were fired.

Zed and Simon Blakely observed the pair leaving. "Stop them, Simon!" yelled Zed.

"Stop them, hell! I'll kill them both, just like I said I would," shouted Simon as he ran to his horse.

Momentarily, all hell broke loose. The camp was alive with action that smacked into everything. The four other outlaws had weapons in hand, firing at the intruders. The air filled with the stench of gunpowder.

One after another, the outlaws took lead and fell to the ground wounded or dead. Within minutes the camp was still. Two men lay dead in a heap in grotesque death while the wounded lay too weak to move.

Shadows loomed over the wounded. There were three men with Silver Stars on their chests. One was a painted Cheyenne.

"Mar-shall Clay. This good fight. We win. Count many coup. Sammy Colter saw the frightened looks on the two wounded men and threw back his head and laughed.

* *

Johanna Stockton and Jamie Patterson reached their horses, mounted quickly and were on the run. Simon Blakely jumped into the saddle, sunk spur to his animal and whipped it into a frenzy of break neck speed.

Johanna and Jamie rode downward toward a road, then stretched out in a fast pace.

Simon Blakely gained on the pair. He rammed his spurs into his mount's flanks so hard that blood ran from the animal's side. He whipped his horse repeatedly with his quirt and yelled at the animal to run faster. Simon reached back and jerked his Winchester from its scabbard. He lined it directly up on Jamie's back and squeezed the trigger. He grinned with dark evil when Jamie pitched forward against his mount's neck, then slid to the ground, his foot still in the right stirrup and was dragged twenty some yards before his boot disengaged from the stirrup. Jamie Patterson lay unmoving on the cold hard ground.

Johanna Stockton was just ahead of Jamie when she heard him grunt with the impact of the rifle slug in his back. She reined in quickly to pull beside and reached out for him. She just missed him as he slid from the saddle.

Johanna reached for the Colt Revolver that Jamie had given her and she pointed it at Simon as he closed the distance toward her. There was a metallic click, followed by five more clicks. Jamie had given her an empty revolver.

Simon Blakely came at her. He had shoved his rifle back into the boot and had drawn his Colt. He fiercely rode straight at her and that Colt in his hand blazed hot lead.

Long furrows of dirt and dust showered up on Johanna as she momentarily stood there wondering what to do. Suddenly, she saw it. Jamie's Colt was still in his holster. Could she make it to him? She had to try. Johanna feinted a run away, then suddenly turned and dashed for Jamie Patterson and the loaded revolver at his belt. Simon once again lined his revolver up on the woman and squeezed the trigger.

* *

Johanna dived to the dirt, then rolled over Jamie's body. She grabbed him by the gun belt and tried to turn his limp body so that she could grasp the revolver and withdraw it from its holster.

Simon's shot split the air and the bullet drove straight through Johanna's right side. She cried out with the hot burn of lead as it knocked her reeling from Jamie's side. Johanna could feel the warm rush of crimson as it spread along her shirt. She tried to get up and crawl back to Jamie and the revolver but found that she was weakening by the moment.

Simon reined in his mount and dismounted. He grinned crookedly and with evil as he once again pointed his revolver at Johanna. This time he would shoot her right between the eyes. He slowly cocked the hammer back, lined up, and squeezed the trigger.

"Click."

Simon had failed to count his shots and now he had to reload. He flipped open the loading gate of his Colt and began to frantically punch out empty shells.

Johanna painfully crawled to Jamie's side once again. With all her might, she rolled him over and slid the Colt from his holster. She lay back breathing hard and laboriously. She looked hard at Simon who had just finished loading his revolver.

Simon laughed wildly at the bleeding and half dazed woman. He taunted her. "Come on, woman. You got Jamie's Colt now. Let me see you use it. Come on now. Point it at me and let's you and I shoot each other."

Johanna struggled to focus her eyes. She lifted the heavy Colt, cocking it in one motion, and leveling it in Simon's direction. She pulled the trigger.

Simon had death in his eyes as he watched the woman struggle with the heavy Colt. He waited until she had almost brought it in line with him when he thrust out his own revolver, hammer cocked back and waiting.

He couldn't help himself. "Goodbye forever, Old Woman."

Three revolver shots split the air as one report.

Johanna saw her shot thud into Simon's left side as dust pillowed up from his grimy shirt. Her eyes widened as Simon's shot smacked into the ground beside her. The third shot pillowed up on Simon's chest—dead center through the breast bone.

Suddenly, five more Colt Revolver shots cracked in succession, each one pillowed up dust on Simon's shirt front almost exactly where the previous bullet had entered his body. Simon's body jerked violently six times and then was slammed back onto the cold hard ground with the final shot. Blood oozed from the six bullet holes that covered only the size of a silver dollar in Simon Blakely's chest. His eyes had rolled back up into his head and his mouth gaped open. His limp and broken body lay grotesque in death.

Johanna Stockton suddenly felt exhausted, but turned slowly to see a darkened figure walk out of the shadows of pine to the side of her. Her eyes misted over and she began to cry softly to herself as she viewed the Silver Star on the shadow's vest.

Cole Stockton stepped softly up to his mother and held his hand out to her. She took it and he lifted her to her feet. They looked deeply into each other's eyes for a long moment. Cole pulled her to his breast and held her tightly as sobs ran through her body.

"You are safe now. Clay, Spotted Hawk, and Sammy--yes, Sammy Colter are all here with us. Come, Mother, we'll get that bullet out of you and take care of you."

"Cole. That young man, lying over there, saved my life. They were going to kill me, but he stopped them. He protected me all along the trip. Be gentle when you bury him. Bury him separate from the rest. He was not among those so mean to the bone with ugliness and hate. Bury him and let me put some wildflowers on his grave."

U.S. Marshal Cole Stockton nodded his understanding to his beloved mother.

Mother and son then turned as one and walked slowly toward the dark colored chestnut horse called Warrior.

CHAPTER SEVEN

Gold Fever

Meanwhile, at Fort Lyon, Colorado, a cavalry sergeant and corporal stood near the stockade wall speaking in low tones.

"Did you see the papers today?" asked Corporal Joseph Smythe to his comrade in arms.

Sergeant Bill Tabor replied, "Yeah, I saw them. There's been another gold strike in the Montana Territory. People are rushing up there seeking gold and we are stuck here in Colorado, minding simple-minded savages on the reservation."

Smythe felt uneasy and looked around them before continuing. The more he talked, the more excited he became, although he kept the volume of his voice low. "We talked of this before. We could be part of that gold strike. We could be rich. All we have to do is get out from the fort and not come back. We could pick up some civilian clothes along the way and trade horses. Damn it, Bill, I'm tired of busting my britches for twenty-three dollars a month. I want to have money. I want beautiful women around me; I want all the whiskey I can drink. I want to go up there and get some of that gold."

"Well, Corporal. We just may have that chance. I traded duty with old Sergeant Whitmore this morning and it seems that the new young lieutenant is being given his first chance at leading our patrol. We are going into the wilds and then north a bit. As I see it, we can hand pick those that want to go with us, and at first chance, leave the lieutenant and go our way."

"What do you mean, leave the lieutenant? You know that he won't just let us go. He'll have us shot!"

"Well, what do you think we are going to do with him?"

"I never thought of killing an officer before, Bill. I don't like it."

"Do you want that gold or not?" snarled Bill Tabor.

"Yes, I want all the gold that I can carry."

"Good! Now, there are eight men in this company that want to go with us. All of them are on the duty roster to ride this here patrol. We will take care of the lieutenant, and then all of us will ride up there and get our share of that gold. Besides, we might need all the help we can get. There are still some hostiles roaming the territory in between that gold and us. Get ready. We will be leaving at five in the morning."

* *

Laura Sumner stirred under her blankets. She yawned and then stretched out her body. She stopped suddenly as her senses caught the familiar aroma of fresh coffee brewing, bacon sizzling, and the sweet smell of hot maple syrup.

She lay there in her bed quietly listening to the muffled sounds of movement in her kitchen. Suddenly, there was a warm wet sensation on her toes. Her eyes went wide and she giggled a bit.

Laura threw open the covers and peered down at her feet.

"I thought so, you little monster. How many times do I have to tell you to not lick my toes in the morning?"

The golden-haired puppy named Lady, squirmed her way up along Laura's body and, reaching her destination, began licking her face. Laura reached for the roly-poly puppy and holding her up in the air, mockingly scolded her. "You little rascal! I ought to stick you in Cole's room after he goes to sleep."

The thought occurred to her. "I wonder what he would do? Him, waking up with a puppy licking his toes. No, I can't do that. He would probably think that you were a snake and shoot you first and ask questions later. Still, I would just like to do it one time. I'll bet that he giggles just like me."

Laura rose from her soft warm bed and pulled on her robe. The puppy sat on the floor right beside her. Laura moved to the door, and

Lady trotted out right behind her, all the way to the front door of the ranch house. Laura opened the door and the puppy dashed out and began sniffing her territory.

Laura walked into the kitchen to find Johanna Stockton all dressed in boots, jeans, and shirt. Johanna was lightly moving all around the kitchen humming merrily to as she minded the bacon, watched the coffee pot, and "flipped" griddlecakes into the air, catching them with the skillet. She was having fun.

Laura shuffled to the small table and sat down. Three settings sat ready. Johanna stepped to her, smiled, and poured coffee into her cup.

"Good morning, Laura. It's a beautiful day, isn't it?"

"Yes, it is. Johanna, why are you up so early? I usually start the fire in the wood stove and fix breakfast for Cole and myself. I don't mind it, but you would think that you would want to rest a bit after the adventurous stagecoach trip you made."

"Well, Laura. I was so excited about being here at your ranch, at being here in Colorado, and I guess about making new friends, that I just couldn't sleep past dawn. I thought that I might as well make myself useful. If you mind it, I won't do it anymore. I'll wait until you rise and then, I'll help you—that is, if you don't mind."

"Well, Johanna, it is a bit different for me. If I seem a little grumpy any morning, just pour me some of that coffee and make me sit and drink it. I'll be all right then."

A happy greeting interrupted the two women, "How's my two best girls this morning?"

Laura and Johanna turned to face Cole Stockton. He had that silly grin on his face and was kind of chuckling to himself. "Put two women together in a kitchen and all hell breaks loose. It's a wonder that a man could get a decent meal around here."

"Bobby Cole Stockton! You watch your tongue. Laura and I are working things out. You'd better watch it, or you can just ride into town and eat there. We'll call the boys in here to sample our breakfast doings, and I bet that we get more respect."

U.S. Marshal Cole Stockton laughed heartily. He knew when he'd been had. He bowed gracefully in the manner of a gay cavalier.

"My apologies, Ma'am! I didn't mean to put you all in such a dither. That coffee smells good. Do you think that a poor, lowly marshal could, perhaps, join you two ladies for a good breakfast?"

Laura was almost in tears as she laughed. Johanna stepped up to Cole and kissed him on the cheek. He blushed a bit, then stepped up to Laura. She raised her smiling face to him and Johanna could feel the warmth of the kiss from across the room.

Johanna smiled silently to herself as she poured her eldest son a cup of steaming hot coffee.

* *

The fifteen-man cavalry patrol had made ten miles from Fort Lyon when they stopped to rest their horses.

Lieutenant Thomas turned to his second in command, "Sergeant, have a small fire built and have the men make coffee."

"Yessir! All right, get a fire going and break out that coffee."

Corporal Smythe stepped up to Sergeant Bill Tabor.

"We maybe got problems. We brought five more men than those that we know are with us. I say that we just take over and leave all trussed up and alive."

"No. We can't do that. We can't leave any witness as to where we are headed. We'll just have to take care of the other troopers as well."

Twenty minutes later, ten murderous deserters rode on their way to the Montana Territory. The bodies of a young lieutenant of cavalry and four troopers lay where the fugitives had shot them, in the back. All was silent.

An hour passed, and then, a low moan. A weak movement of an arm. More time passed. A young man rolled over and lay facing the afternoon sun. Pain shot through his body as he tried to move. His mouth was dry, his lips parched. He mouthed silent words heard only by the tiny inhabitants of the wilds as he opened his tunic and slowly pulled out a small ledger and pencil.

He fought off the nausea and darkness as he painfully wrote the few words. Then, with a final breath, he passed into a world filled with gentle love. The young lieutenant was dead.

* *

Cole Stockton, Laura Sumner, and Johanna Stockton sat in the small kitchen enjoying breakfast and each other's company when the front door opened and Judd Ellison, Laura's foreman, tramped across the main room to stick his head into the kitchen and make mock sniffing motions.

"Gee Miss Laura, that coffee and bacon sure smells good."

All three at the table laughed.

"All right, Judd, come and drag up a chair. Help yourself to some coffee and grab up a plate from the cupboard. There's plenty to go around."

"Miss Laura, I got my hands on a newspaper yesterday and spent the night reading it. You, of course, know about the supposed gold strike up in the Montana Territory. Well, I was just thinking. Miners need horses and we've a plenty to sell. I was thinking that someone ought to ride on up there and make some deals—perhaps for a couple of hundred head. I'll bet that we could make a tidy sum iffen we were the first to promise some good horses up that way."

Laura pondered the thought. She couldn't argue with that thought. They had over five hundred head of broke-to-saddle horses to sell, and no time like the present to make a true profit. There would be money for "extra" things.

"Alright, Judd. If you will watch the ranch for a week or so, I and Johanna will ride up that way and see what deals we can strike up."

Cole sat thoughtful for a long moment. "You know, I think that I'll just ride along. It's been a while since I rode through that country, and there may be need of the law. Besides, two women on horseback in the wilds between here and there? I know that you two can take care of yourselves pretty good but, I would feel a whole lot better if I were along."

"Yeah, Cole. We know. There are wild Indians, outlaws, and the vast elements of nature itself," admitted Johanna.

"Yes. That is what I was thinking," agreed Laura.

"All right, Cole. You can come with us. In fact, it might be right nice to have someone that we can pick on all the way up to Montana," smirked Laura.

"Oh Lordy! Maybe I will change my mind and stay around here," Cole feinted doubt.

"Oh No, Cole! You opened your mouth and put your two cents in the pot. Now, you will escort your two favorite girls to the mining camps of Montana. We'll leave this very afternoon."

* *

Ten deserters rode slowly through the Lower Colorado wilds. They picked their way through unfamiliar territory and, at times, found thick stands of forest and heavy bushes in their way. They had to backtrack and work their way around in order to stay headed in a northerly direction.

They also looked for other things, namely, the opportunity to change clothes, acquire gun belts and exchange horses. Until they could do that, they would stand out like a sore thumb.

Sergeant Bill Tabor spoke to his companion, Corporal Smythe, "Look for signs of a settler cabin. They would be the first choice to change these uniforms, and besides, settlers are usually far out from any visitors and it may be weeks before anyone discovers them."

"You're not thinking of killing again, are you?" asked Joseph with dread in his voice.

"Don't worry about it, Smythe. If you don't have the stomach for it, I'll do it. Remember, we can't leave any witnesses to our trail."

"I just don't like the killing. There may be a woman with any settler cabin we come across. I don't hold with killing women. They'd hunt us down and hang us for sure if we killed a woman."

"I'll tell you what, Smythe. Should we run across some women, me and the rest of the boys will have our fun and you can just wait with the horses. That way, you can ease your mind that you didn't have anything to do with it." Tabor's contempt for Smythe coated his words.

Worry consumed Corporal Smythe now. All he wanted to do was get away and get to the gold strike up around Helena, Montana. He could get lost in those mountains and after accumulating enough gold, he would make for California and start a new life. Bill Tabor was a killer.

Smythe thought more about it. He should have known. He had seen Tabor in action against various Indians, and Tabor was extremely vicious. On more than one occasion, Smythe had seen some wounded Indians attempt to surrender. Tabor had only grinned and then shot them right between the eyes. He had a brilliant gleam to his eyes when he killed them, and Smythe groaned with the memory.

They had gone ten miles further when the deserter band saw the thin trail of wood smoke rising up through the trees. They spread out in a long line resembling a cavalry charge formation and rode cautiously toward the smoke.

* *

Leonard Cates and his wife sat in front of the fireplace when the door to their cabin suddenly burst open and the group of uniformed scavengers rushed into the room, revolvers drawn.

Cates jumped up and was immediately shot dead by two of the deserters. Ellen Cates screamed and tried to reach her husband. Three men rushed to her, grabbed her roughly and began to rip off her clothes. She screamed and tried to fight them every inch of the way, until finally, someone slammed a fist into her mouth and she passed out. They took their pleasure.

Others entered the cabin and milled around grinning as they waited their turn with the woman. Some of the men ransacked the cabin, trying on all of the dead husband's clothes.

They ripped open the cupboards and, finding tins of food, filled some burlap bags with everything that they could carry.

Finally, when everyone was satisfied, Bill Tabor walked up to the sweat stained and defiled woman, grinned at her with an evil smile and casually shot her between the eyes. He turned to exit the cabin. As an afterthought, he went to the fireplace, withdrew a burning brand and set fire to everything that would burn.

The ten men rode silently away. Only one looked back. Corporal Smythe's eyes grew dark and worried as brilliant flames consumed the cabin and ominous black smoke rose heavily into the air. Smythe found himself praying for the souls of the people in the cabin. He now wished that he had never consented to join Tabor and this group. He wished that he were back at Fort Lyon on some mundane duty.

CHAPTER EIGHT

A Path of Murder and Destruction

Cole Stockton stepped out to the porch as Jud Ellison and Juan Soccorro walked across the ranch yard leading saddled Warrior, Mickey, and Brandy. Wrangler Mike Thompson was a few yards behind them with a packhorse outfitted for two weeks on the trail.

"Thanks, Judd. I thought those gals would never stop talking. You know I like to saddle my own horse."

"That's all right, Cole. I figured to save you some time. Warrior is raring to go somewhere. He could hardly stand still waiting to get that bridle and saddle on him."

Cole stepped down from the porch and stroked Warrior's face and neck. "So, you want to take a ride, huh? Well, we are going to take a long, long ride Boy. I trust that you are up to it. That is, as soon as Mother and Laura get out here."

The door opened and both Johanna and Laura emerged. Cole looked at them and the thought struck him, "They are like two peas in a pod. They dress alike, act alike, and think alike. Lord help me."

Laura wore her normal apparel of boots, spurs, jeans, dark blue shirt, yellow neckerchief, and "lucky" black Stetson. Johanna wore boots, spurs, jeans, dark blue shirt, red neckerchief, and dark brown Stetson. Both women had gun belts slung around their slim waists in a knowing manner. Both carried their Winchester rifles, which they slid into scabbards when they stepped up to their horses. The next thing that they did, and they were like twins, was to throw a stirrup up over the saddle horn and check the chinches. They both spoke softly to their mounts as they stroked long sleek necks and shoulders.

Cole grinned with amusement. He waited for a few moments before announcing, "As soon as you horsewomen are ready, we can start this arduous trek into the wilds." The women looked at him for a moment, then put boot to stirrup and swung into their saddles. Cole followed suit and taking the lead rope to the packhorse, turned toward the gate of the Sumner Ranch. Laura and Johanna followed close behind, both talking pleasantly.

* *

Spotted Hawk had been an important warrior of his tribe during the earlier years. Now, in his late forties, his band had taken to the reservation to live in peace. Although agreeable to peace with the white man, he still craved the adventure of wild trails. As such, he had volunteered himself as a scout for the U.S. Army.

During this time that Cole, Laura, and Johanna had begun their trip, Spotted Hawk worked his way through the wilds toward Fort Lyon when he came upon the military death scene. He found the five dead men, all soldiers, no others and read the signs. He put together the story in his mind after only Army shod hoof prints at the scene.

"Other soldiers shoot these men and ride off toward the great mountains. Why?"

Spotted Hawk was checking the bodies when he found the half-written note that young Lieutenant Thomas had scribbled.

"Sergeant Tabor—10 men—shot—deserters."

Spotted Hawk could not read the white man's paper, but he knew that it was important. He buried the five men as best that he could and taking the officer's ledger with him, mounted his pony and struck out for Fort Lyon. He would deliver Lieutenant Thomas' last message.

* *

Within a day's ride, the deserter group came across three cowboys sitting around a campfire for afternoon coffee. Within minutes all three cowboys lay dead and the scavengers were changing horses, clothes and gun belts.

Bill Tabor grinned. They kept getting lucky. A few more situations like this and the entire group would be outfitted like civilians. Besides, he was enjoying the killing. It gave him a sense of power. Plans formed in Tabor's mind. Prospecting for gold was backbreaking work. He and his men would get their gold the "easy" way. They would take it from those who had it.

"Who knows?" he thought "Maybe we can make some prospectors disappear and file on their claims. It would make us look respectable and provide a reason for all the gold we will be exchanging for cash money."

The group of ten horsemen rode slowly away from this scene as the ashes of three uniforms lay in the bed of the campfire.

* *

Tabor decided to split his group into two factions. One would ride east and then north, gathering up goods and supplies as they went. His group would ride west and then north doing likewise. They would meet at a point fifty miles north and continue the journey to Montana as a single group.

A freighting outfit next suffered the wrath of Bill Tabor and his group. The two wagons and four men had camped for the evening when five men rode out of the trees.

The wagon boss stood up as they rode up to the camp. Tabor sat his horse grinning at him. Without warning, he drew his revolver and shot the man dead. The other wagon men, caught completely by surprise, all lay dead and stripped of their clothes in the late afternoon sun.

"Well, now," said Tabor to his men, "we've got some valuable merchandise here. Bury those guys and in the morning, we will become freighters. We'll drive these wagons up to Montana and sell the stuff. No one will be looking for a freight outfit. They'll be looking for a large group of riders." He chuckled with the idea.

In the meantime, the second group of five men came upon two small homesteads. No one was home at the first, so they ransacked the house and took everything that they could carry. The second homestead was owned by two men who were partners. Their fate was sealed by .45 caliber lead, and the house was burned down around their stripped bodies.

The deserters rode off with all of the horses, clothing, food supplies, guns, and ammunition.

By a miracle of fate, the scheduled Denver stagecoach passed unmolested within one hundred yards of the five man group.

Tom Skinner argued that they should take the coach also as it might be carrying gold shipments, or at the very least, an Express pouch of considerable currency.

Corporal Smythe breathed a bit easier. He didn't want to kill anyone, and he felt that he might have saved some people's lives by not allowing an attack on the coach. He was right.

* *

Cole Stockton led the small procession slowly through the wilds. He pointed out the beauty of nature along the way. They saw mule-ear deer, elk, a brown bear, two eagles on the wing, a red fox, a skunk, and even a few wolves. The wildlife was inspiring.

Johanna felt fascinated with the scenery, even though the going was slow. Amazingly, Cole seemed to know every hidden path through the wilds.

They traveled through thickets, up scenic inclines, around deadfalls, down through invisible tunnels within seemingly solid rock walls, around massive boulders, and into low stream crossings.

He took them upstream, riding within the clear babbling creek water, up and over grassy embankments, and through thick stands of pine and aspen. They crossed small clearings with grasses as high as their stirrups. Massive brown dots became small groups of buffalo as they drew closer.

The sun had begun to fade over the western ridges of the Rocky Mountains when Cole drew up in a clump of pines. He dismounted and motioned for Laura and Johanna to do likewise.

"We'll make camp here and get an early start in the morning. If you ladies will unsaddle the horses and rub them down a bit, I'll gather some wood and start a fire."

Cole stripped off the packhorse and retrieved the coffeepot. He had deliberately paralleled a small creek and now he went down to the stream and filled the pot with clear, cold water. There also, he found dried driftwood and broken branches. He noticed some dead logs along the way. He would return for them.

Within half an hour, a small fire flickered gaily and the coffeepot was on. There was only a thin trail of wood-smoke that rose into the overhanging pine boughs and dissipated.

Laura made biscuits while Johanna cut potatoes and scallions and impaled them on sharp sticks for broiling. Cole took his hunting knife and went back down to the stream. Within an hour, he returned with a makeshift pole and five nice-sized trout. These were placed on forked sticks and set to bake around the campfire.

It was cool enough in the mountains at night and the campfire was kept low enough for warmth, but not to advertise a campsite. Laura and Johanna rolled up in their blankets and almost immediately fell asleep. Cole leaned back against a tree somewhat back from the fire and took the first watch. He would wake Laura in three hours so she could relieve him.

Cole was alone with his own thoughts as he watched the two women sleep. He listened for the obvious sounds—sounds of small nocturnal creatures scurrying through the underbrush, the hoot of an owl, the low moaning cry of the wolf. These sounds signaled that all was right with the world. Had they not been there, danger would be close at hand.

Cole glanced up at the moon casting its illuminating glow upon the land. He thought of those many times that he had sat alone by a small fire wishing that Laura was by his side. He smiled with the thought, and his eyes turned soft as he watched Laura sleep.

The morning came quietly over the ridges to the east. Laura stretched and opened her eyes to look at Cole. He was still sitting by the tree and smiling at her with a sheepish look about him. She could feel the warmth of his heart as she looked deep into his eyes. She felt the stirring within her own senses as silently, unto each other, they spoke their feelings.

Johanna wakened to the aroma of fresh coffee and bacon frying. Cole was saddling the horses. Suddenly, he stopped and listened intently. The horses' ears had pricked up.

Someone was coming towards them. A lot of riders were coming their way up through the trees.

Cole moved to his Winchester and held it at the ready. Johanna took up hers also, as did Laura. They spread out a bit and waited.

The first glimpse of the approaching group showed that the riders wore uniforms of the U.S. Cavalry.

* *

Cole watched as the three point troopers rode slowly toward them. A larger body of cavalry emerged from the trees and also moved toward them.

"H-a-l-l-o the camp!" sounded one of the point troopers.

"Come on in!" replied Cole.

The troopers approached. The senior point trooper spoke, "Sir, we are looking for a stream located very near here to water our horses. Have you seen it?"

"Yes, Corporal. It's just down the slope over there."

"Thank you, Sir. My Captain may want to ask you some questions. He will be right up."

Momentarily, the captain and his guidon bearer reined their mounts in front of Cole.

"Good morning, Sir. I am Captain Starrett from Fort Lyon."

"Good morning, Captain. This is Miss Laura Sumner of the Sumner Ranch, and this is my Mother, Johanna Stockton. I am Cole Stockton, the United States Marshal for this territory."

"Marshal Stockton, we have ridden most of the night and are in search of a party of ten deserters. They murdered their officer along with four other troopers and rode toward this way. This, of course, is a military matter at this point, but have you seen any such body of men?"

"No, Captain. We have seen no one but you so far. Things being as they are, I would imagine that they might be headed for the recent gold rush in Montana. We are headed that way also, and will keep a look out for them."

"Perhaps we can ride together for a while, Marshal. My orders are to bring them back dead or alive to stand Courts Martial for their actions."

Laura Sumner spoke up, "Yes, Captain. We'd like the company. It's not often that two women get escorted by an entire troop of cavalry. It is very gallant of you to offer."

Thirty minutes later Cole, Laura, and Johanna rode out beside Captain Starrett and his troop.

They rode slowly toward the north, always looking for sign of a group of horsemen. Close to Noon Cole spotted some tracks. He pulled up and dismounted to study them.

"Captain, I think I've found their trail. There were at least ten horses in this group that rode through here. It looks to be about late afternoon yesterday. If it is them, they are headed north to Montana."

They rode further, following the trail. Two hours later, the smell of charred wood was strong in their nostrils. Captain Starrett halted the troop.

Cole Stockton, Captain Starrett, and eight troopers rode to the site. They found the charred remains of the Cates cabin, with the violated and burned bodies of Leonard and Ellen.

Captain Starrett had his men bury the couple. Cole somberly turned to the Captain and announced, "Now, it is murder, rape, and pillage of civilians. I want those men myself now and there will be hell to pay."

Captain Starrett looked at Stockton's face, and saw the stark stare of death. An icy cold quiver ran down his spine. He had heard before that some gunmen could look straight into the soul of a man and had passed off those stories as folly. Now, he believed them. This man, Cole Stockton, was death itself and the fires of hell burned deep within his being.

CHAPTER NINE

Fate of the Deserters

The deserter bands once again joined together and now crossed into Wyoming Territory. The landscape gradually changed from mountains and forests to open rolling hills. This land was cattle country.

When the men were hungry, they killed branded cattle along the way. Not surprisingly, they only took the best cuts, leaving the carcass to the scavengers.

At one point, they crossed paths with a flock of sheep. Bill Tabor shot and killed the two herders just for fun, and then most of the group who had no use for sheep, slaughtered the entire sheep herd. They laughed and joked as they worked the levers of their rifles. They even made bets with each other as to what type of shot they would make to kill the sheep.

Bit by bit, the two stolen freight wagons filled up with plunder. They lived off the wares taken from those they raped and murdered. Farmhouses were left devastated and burned. Bodies lay as they left them, naked, mutilated and dead.

The deserters thought themselves invincible. They looked forward to working the Montana gold fields. They were all going to be rich, the easy way, by taking their gold from those that worked hard for it.

A week passed and the deserters breathed easier. They now believed that they had completely disappeared from the grasp of the Army and the law.

Little did they realize that taking the heavy freight wagons had slowed them somewhat, and that a column of cavalry and a United States Marshal kept gaining on them.

The shape of the land changed considerably as they got closer to Montana. The land sloped gradually uphill and travel became more difficult with the wagons.

Tabor refused to abandon the wagons. He wanted those goods and supplies to support their initial stay in Montana. He drove his men to that end.

Corporal Smythe grew more worried each day. Tabor was becoming even more irritable. He could be vicious when provoked and some of the men began to keep their distance.

Things came to a head one afternoon. Tabor called the men to him and laid it out straight. "There's those of you that feel inclined to leave this outfit. Now's your chance. Speak up and we'll talk it out."

Jeff Carnes stepped forward. "Sarge, there's a few of us that would like to just ride on up to the gold country. We aim to find and work a claim like anybody else up there. We don't lay claim to any of the goods in them wagons. You can have them. We just want to go."

"Sure thing, Carnes," said Tabor. He drew his revolver and shot Carnes three times straight in the middle. Carnes jerked violently with each thud of the .44 lead, and slammed to the ground to lie in a grotesque heap. His empty eyes stared toward the big sky.

Tabor stood with smoking revolver in hand, "Now, anyone else want to leave this outfit? I said from the first that we are all in this together until all of us get rich. Any man who feels that he wants to leave, can drag iron with me."

And then, Tabor laughed like a crazy man and waved his Colt menacingly along the group. He fancied himself as a gunfighter, and he wanted to prove it.

* *

The cavalry troop found itself nearing the end of its supplies. One morning, Captain Starrett turned to Cole Stockton and advised him, "Marshal, we have to ride into Fort Laramie and re-supply. My men and I will angle from there and hope to join with you again about fifty miles further north. Also, I failed to mention that there is another cavalry troop working its way parallel to us. They would have an Indian scout with them and should intercept us somewhere a bit north of the Rosebud Creek. That scout was the one who found the remains of Lieutenant Thomas and the unfortunate troopers. It was he who brought word of the murders and desertion."

The cavalry troop peeled off from the small group, and once again there was Cole Stockton, Laura Sumner, and Johanna Stockton riding alone on the vast Wyoming prairie.

Within five more miles, they came across the remains of the murdered sheep men and slaughtered stock.

Cole sat Warrior and just looked. Laura and Johanna sat their saddles and shook their heads. This scene was senseless killing. These people were worse than any scavengers they had ever witnessed. These men killed for the shear fun of it.

Laura could see it in Cole's eyes. She could feel the intensity of the man's determination. He wanted these men and he wanted them bad. He was going to catch up with them and there would be blood on the ground, deserter blood.

* *

The Stockton party continued onward. It was five hours later that they found the remains of Jeffrey Carnes. Vultures were ripping flesh when Cole, Laura, and Johanna each squeezed off with their Winchesters. Three giant birds of prey jerked in mid-air with the impact of .44-40 lead, feathers flying everywhere. The remainder of the predators took to the air and continued to circle in wait.

Cole looked down upon the corpse. "They killed one of their own men."

"How can you tell, Cole?" asked Johanna.

"Well, they didn't strip this one like all the others. That means to me that he was one of their own. Secondly, look at his boots. He's wearing cavalry boots. Looks like he either couldn't find the right size from others, or he just couldn't bear to part with those that were most comfortable to him. My next guess is that they've got some disagreement amongst them. That may work out to my advantage. Another thing, we are gaining on them. By the condition of the dead man, we are only about four hours behind them."

Johanna spoke up, "Cole, you're not thinking of a hard ride just to catch up with them, are you? I mean, there has got to be at least nine men in that group. Shouldn't you wait until that Army troop catches up to us before you press them?"

"Mother, ten against one is one thing, but ten against three trail hardened Deputy U.S. Marshals is another. Both of you raise your right hands and repeat after me, I do solemnly swear that I will uphold the laws of the Constitution of the United States of America, and that I will—so help me God."

Laura and Johanna swore in and Cole handed each a Deputy U.S. Marshal's Star to pin on their shirt fronts.

"Good! Now, both of you frontier women are my Deputy Marshals. Let's ride and ride hard. I want those men and I want to get as many as I can before that cavalry troop rejoins with us. I know that all of the deserters aren't killers. I just want those that are. Once they are in my custody, those Army boys will have to wait until Judge Wilkerson gets finished with them. I aim to see the killers hang for their deeds—or bury them where I find them."

The posse of three began a grueling ride. Warrior, Mickey, and Brandy stretched out in a mile-eating run. They paced with their one limiting factor, the packhorse. Laura Sumner's determination to have the best horses in Colorado was paying off. The packhorse had speed, stamina, and kept up fairly well considering the weight that it carried.

They galloped for half an hour, walked for half an hour, galloped for half an hour, stopped and rested for half an hour, then galloped again. The pace was steady and designed to save the horses as much as possible.

Mile after mile fell away and darkness began to fall. Cole finally relented and let them set up a cold camp for a few hours. No fire was built, for the glow might be seen for several miles.

The trio unsaddled their horses and unpacked the packhorse to let them graze a bit. They huddled with their blankets around themselves, ate dried beef jerky and cold biscuits. They drank cold canteen water.

Laura looked deep into Cole's eyes. The flame of justice burned bright. He looked deep into her crystal blue eyes and there was companionship. She had often visualized what it would be like on a hot trail with Cole. Now, she was finding out. She found that she was becoming even closer to him, in mind, in heart, and in soul.

Johanna quietly watched both of them and knew what was happening. She smiled silently as the radiating heat of their thoughts warmed the air like no mere campfire could do.

Cole and Laura, even though of one mind before, were fusing their souls into a partnership of unprecedented admiration and love. There was no denying the presence of eternal devotion.

Laura moved closer to Cole and they sat together, his arm around her, hand in hand, a determined aura about them. Johanna looked away, a sudden flash of remembrance of times before, and a small tear rolled down her dusty cheek. She took a deep breath and whispered the name…"Flint." The image was momentary, but the warmth spread throughout her entire body. Johanna seemed to glow with her memories as light.

Four hours later, they mounted and continued the pursuit. Cole suspected that the deserters would camp for the night, and he thought right. Dawn began as a gradual lighting in the eastern sky. The rays of the morning sun had not quite peeked over the land when the small posse caught glimpse of a flickering glow in the distance. Could it be a large campfire?

* *

The Stockton posse rode steadily toward the flickering glow until the morning sun cast its warming rays upon the land. They rode more warily then, as the campers, whoever they might be, would be stirring now.

The tree-dotted slopes told Cole Stockton that they had passed into or were very near to the Montana Territory. The campsite in question rested under a stand of pine facing an open field of grasses. There was no way to approach without being detected.

Cole, Laura, and Johanna lay on their stomachs at the crest of a small hill watching the early morning activities of the campers. Laura spoke first, "Cole, this looks like a bunch of wagon freighters. We could probably get a good cup of coffee if we just rode right on over there."

Cole replied, "Maybe, maybe not. I want to watch them for a while more. I have a feeling about them, and the hair on the back of my neck is standing straight up. I feel evil in that camp, an evil of great magnitude. Besides, there are too many men for the number of wagons they've got with them to be a freight outfit. Count them. There are at least nine men in that group. I don't see a uniform amongst them, but they've been taking the clothes off the people they killed. I think they did it just to get different clothing. They wanted no witnesses as to their trail, so they killed each and every one. What they did was to leave a trail of naked bodies."

The "posse" watched as the freight wagons readied for the day's journey. Cole watched with intense interest. "These men are not freighters."

"O.K., Cole. Just how do you know that?"

"Look at how they are positioned. These men are cavalrymen. Look at how they ride two by two and three by three. Freighters have no formation. They "mingle" as they ride. These men are the men we are looking for."

"What are you going to do, Cole?"

"Well, you saw how they camped. They were fairly well barricaded in and had a good field of fire. They probably did that out of habit. Whoever is in charge knows his business about defense of a position, as would a Sergeant of the Cavalry. This will take some thinking. In the meantime, we will follow them at about a mile back. I want to be within a short time of taking them."

A solemn thought crossed Cole's mind, "By the way, Laura, Mother. If those boys run across anyone else on the trail and, well, if we hear gunfire, I intend to ride straight in there and shoot whatever is standing. I will not stand by and let them kill another person, if I can help it."

There was no argument from Johanna and Laura.

The deserters packed up the wagons and slowly rolled northward. They had gone but a few miles when they happened upon a ranch wagon. John and Trish Williams with their three small children were returning from a trading post with monthly staples when they saw the freight wagons bearing toward them. They pulled off to the side of the wagon road to let the heavy laden wagons pass.

John Williams had himself been in the freight business before and he watched the oncoming wagons with great interest. Something was not right. These men drove the freight wagons like they didn't know their teams. Any freighter knows his team and speaks to them as he drives. These drivers only knew how to crack the whip and slap-the-reins.

Williams reflected on this fact, as well as the newspaper accounts of "a group of Army deserters" from Fort Lyon in Colorado. A sense of danger crossed his mind as the lead three horsemen of the freighter outfit suddenly broke into a gallop toward them.

Williams immediately grabbed his whip and cracked it above his two-horse team's heads. The horses turned the wagon back toward the trading post at a fast run.

* *

Bill Tabor rode in the lead. He had seen the small ranch wagon and realized that there was only a man, a woman, and three small children. His wicked mind saw yet another killing and another woman to be had—a woman to be raped and, when she begged for her life, he could put a bullet in her brain.

He wanted the woman for himself and for his men. The children would be killed outright. He had no use for children. He thought, perhaps his men would settle down some if they had another woman to ravage.

Tabor signaled his group of men forward. They broke into a hard gallop. They would ride right up to the wagon; Tabor would shoot the man and children in front of the woman. His men would drag the woman out of the wagon and have her right there. He relished in the thought.

Suddenly, the wagon turned and was running all out, back the way that it had come. Tabor became furious. He yelled to his men, "They're running away. Let's show them what true cavalrymen can do. Catch them! Shoot the horses if you must, but I want that wagon! I want that woman! Let's go!"

The three deserters whipped their horses into a full run. They were gaining on the wagon. They drew their revolvers and fired at the wagon in hopes of slowing them down, in hopes of hitting either the driver or one of the horses.

* *

Cole Stockton and his "posse" heard the firing ahead of the wagons. Cole turned briefly in the saddle and yelled, "That's it! I'm going up there."

He heeled Warrior into a gallop, then stretched out into a full run toward the freight wagons. He slid his Winchester out of its scabbard, then leaned forward in the saddle as he urged Warrior into a death defying run for life.

Laura looked at Johanna. Silent words passed between them. Both women drew Winchesters and levered a bullet into the chamber. As one, they lightly raked spurs to Mickey and Brandy. Both horses immediately burst into a full gallop. They were both Deputy U.S. Marshals and, by God, they were going to support Cole. They trailed Cole by almost a half-mile. Cole was riding full out.

Laura and Johanna watched as Cole reached the rear-most riders of the "freight outfit." He raced past them, and it took them by surprise.

Suddenly, the rear-most men drew rifles and leveled them at Cole; they rapidly shot at him. Puffs of powder smoke lifted from their rifles as they fired toward the racing Marshal.

Suddenly, hot molten rifle lead slammed into the rear of the column. Two men jolted off their horses. The deserter group pulled up sharp and turned to face two horsemen—rather, two determined horsewomen riding hell bent toward them with Winchesters spitting death and destruction.

The seasoned cavalrymen tried to hold their line, but without the steady urging of a sergeant or corporal, they broke and began to scatter. Laura rode straight toward the center of the group. She emptied her Winchester, shoved it back into her boot, then with the blur of her right hand, produced her Colt Lightning revolver and began to take a deadly toll.

The drivers halted their wagons. The two men on each box seat dived underneath the heavy wagons and began to fire wildly at Johanna and Laura. Johanna rode wide and to the right of the wagons. Suddenly, she did something that surprised even Laura. Johanna let out with the wildest "Comanche" war cry that anyone had ever heard, then slid to the side of her mount, Brandy, holding on by only a foot and one hand. She slid down and fired her Colt Revolver underneath and in front of Brandy's thundering shoulders.

Johanna was riding just like a wild Comanche warrior. Laura thought to herself, "If she can do that, so can I!" Laura rode to the left of the wagons and slid to the left-hand side of Mickey. She held on by one foot across Mickey's rump and one hand to the saddle horn. She fired her Colt over the saddle, hidden by Mickey's body.

Laura found herself in a state of exhilaration. All of a sudden, she opened her mouth and screamed her version of the wildest "Comanche" war cry that she could imagine.

There they went, riding fast and furious, shooting over the horses and encircling the wagons. The deserters, all dived under the wagons, fired haphazardly at them. Dirt blossomed up all around the two wild women as they rode around the wagons keeping the men pinned down.

* *

Cole Stockton urged Warrior to breakneck speed. He passed the wagons and suddenly hot lead whistled past his left ear, then his right ear. He almost felt the burn as a heavy round passed through his shirt.

Cole headed straight for the front of the wagons when he saw the party ahead of him. He observed the ranch wagon running in a swirl of dirt and dust, and he saw the three men ahead of him riding hard to catch the ranch wagon. He saw them fire at the wagon.

Cole leveled his Winchester at the rear most man. He squeezed off. The man lurched forward, then backward, then tumbled off his horse. The rider next to him turned to look back. He jerked his mount to a halt, turned his horse and leveled his rifle at Stockton. Stockton immediately shot him through the middle before the man could fully line up and fire. The man jerked in the saddle and slumped forward, wounded.

Cole spoke urgently to Warrior. The sturdy Chestnut surged forward even faster.

There was now only one deserter in pursuit of the ranch wagon. Bill Tabor had only one thing on his mind, up to this point. Get that wagon! Something was amiss. Tabor turned in the saddle to find a stranger riding hard to catch him, and the stranger was throwing hot lead.

Tabor made his decision. He meant to kill this intrusive stranger. He reined in his mount sharply, pulled up his horse and dismounted. Standing in wait of the pursuer, Tabor intended to prove his ability as a gunfighter.

Cole Stockton saw the move, and pulling up on Warrior, thought, "So, that's the way he wants it. So be it!"

Stockton slowed Warrior to a walk within thirty yards of Tabor. He turned Warrior to the side and kept him in front of him as he dismounted. He stepped out from his horse and walked toward Tabor, shouting "U.S. Marshal! You are under arrest for murder, rape, stock theft, arson, and whatever else I can think up. You can drag iron, and I sorely hope you do, or you can drop your weapons and come peaceably. It don't matter which way to me. You draw on me, I intend to kill you."

Tabor strutted out in front, his hand hovering over his revolver butt. He snarled at the Marshal. He planned to kill this lawman and leave his bones for the vultures, just like Carnes and the rest.

"Take me if you can, Marshal. You ain't never seen the likes of me! I'm going to shoot you stone cold dead!"

Tabor then made the biggest mistake of his evil life. He touched the butt of his revolver. His hand grasped the black grips of his pistol and it slipped out of his holster. He thought he was looking straight into the eyes of the next man he was going to kill.

Tabor's revolver was almost out of the leather when the first round spun deep into his chest. He jerked back and stared down at the bright red stain. He coughed. He looked further down; his revolver was not even out of the holster. He raised it and, with mouth and eyes open wide, tried to level it at the Marshal.

The second bullet took him in the throat and he choked on his own blood. The third slammed into his belly and it felt like the fires of hell as it burned through his spine. He sank limply to the ground, his unfeeling legs folding underneath him. A fourth bullet tipped the edge of his black heart and the fifth sounded as an ugly thunk as it smacked right between his eyes.

"Bloody Bill Tabor" as his men called him, jerked straight backward and crashed to the ground. His Revolver had never fired a single shot. His eyes stared lifelessly skyward as his evil soul met with the Angel of Eternal Fire.

Sergeant Bill Tabor lay broken, bloody, and stone cold dead, shot to doll rags by a man he planned to prove his ability against. Tabor had been vicious in Indian warfare, and vicious in killing innocent people, but he was no match for a seasoned gunfighter willing to stand against odds and take lead.

Cole Stockton tied Bill Tabor's body over his saddle, and ran a rope from Tabor's horse to his saddle horn. He led out back toward the freight wagons.

Rapid gunfire crackled in the distance.

* *

Captain Starrett and Lieutenant Leyland with their two troops of cavalry had joined together and were approaching the Montana Territory.

Spotted Hawk came galloping wildly toward them, waving his arms for immediate attention. Then, they heard it—gunfire in the distance. It sounded like a small war being waged.

The Indian scout reached the two columns and, with wild exaggerations of his hands and broken English, quickly told the two officers about the sight that he had witnessed. Two galloping wild warriors had two freight wagons and their deserters pinned down.

"Much shooting. Two wild horsemen ride around wagons, make war cries, shoot deserters."

Captain Starrett turned to his command. "Forward, at the Gallop! Y-O-O-O-O!"

* *

Corporal Smythe had been left in charge of the two freight wagons. Everything happened at once. Tabor galloped off in pursuit of a racing ranch wagon, a lone rider galloped past the wagons, chasing Tabor, and the rider was levering his Winchester at Tabor and his two men. Two wildly screaming horsemen raced up to his rear and began shooting his men. The deserter's saddle mounts bolted and ran off. Smythe was confused.

He ordered his men off the wagons for a defensive position. The two riders ringed his position, riding wildly and he could swear that they yelled out Comanche war cries. Bullets smacked into the wagons and into his men. Dirt furrowed up all around them. These riders were deadly.

The terrified deserters were quite shaken with the suddenness of events and it threw their normally steady manner off guard. They fired wildly at the two horsemen, jerking their rounds instead of squeezing them off calmly. They stayed pinned down. They couldn't move the wagons, and they couldn't run.

In spite of the danger, Laura and Johanna were having the time of their lives. They rode hard and furious, screaming at the top of their lungs, and firing hot lead into the wagons and the defenders. Suddenly, Johanna yelled out that she was short of ammunition. Laura also found that she was running short. Something had to break and soon. She wished that Cole would hurry back to the wagons.

The din of battle was suddenly split by the stirring "C" notes of a cavalry trumpet sounding the "Charge." The deserters, as well as Johanna and Laura stopped their firing and watched as two troops of cavalry thundered over the rise and streaked toward them.

Corporal Smythe saw just how futile the situation was. He ordered his remaining men to drop their weapons and stand up with hands held high. He waved a white rag high in the air. He surrendered.

A sigh of relief exhaled from Smythe's lips. He wanted to hunt gold, but he had never envisioned the magnitude of death and destruction that Bill Tabor would lead them through. He felt relieved that it was finally over. Within fifteen minutes, the deserter remnants were in chains and guarded by troopers. The deserters couldn't believe their eyes. They had been stopped in their tracks and bested by two women.

Spotted Hawk, himself seemed amazed that these two women rode and fought like warriors. He paid them special tribute by giving each of them an eagle claw and rawhide thong necklace from his saddlebags. Both women proudly displayed them.

Cole Stockton rode back into the wagon area with a body tied face down over the saddle: Bill Tabor.

Cole surmised the situation, "Well, Captain Starrett, you got your men, and I got the man responsible for this trail of blood. I'll let you have all the live ones for courts-martial. Bury this scavenger Tabor right here in the middle of nowhere in an unmarked grave. His black soul can listen to the moan of wolves and coyotes for the rest of eternity."

Thus, ended the trail of blood. The surviving deserters were returned in chains to Fort Lyon to stand trial, and the Cole Stockton "posse" disbanded to continue on to the gold fields around Helena, Montana. Laura Sumner made some very good deals for all five hundred head of her broken-to-saddle horses, and it looked like good times ahead.

Cole put his arms around Laura and Johanna and hugged them both. "Best two deputies I ever had, somewhat wild and wooley, though. They all laughed as they strode arm in arm down Main Street of Helena, turning in at the nearest restaurant for dinner and hot coffee.

CHAPTER TEN

Milo Jergens

Mike Wilkes looked lovingly at the young woman called Nancy by her friends. Mike was Laura Sumner's youngest wrangler, and it was Saturday, the wrangler's day off.

Mike was of slender build, tall, with dark brown hair and light brown eyes. Mike's hands, typical of a horse wrangler, felt callused and rough from the daily chores of roping and riding the wild ones.

At a casual glance, an observer wouldn't believe that Mike was very strong, but the muscles of his arms were like steel springs.

Today, he wore faded, rumpled jeans with slightly down-trodden boots and tarnished metal spurs. His faded red homespun shirt included a faded red and white polka-dot bandana hung loosely around his neck. Mike always wore his hat pushed slightly back on his head when in town and a shock of his dark hair always seemed to need brushed out of his eyes.

When he entered the saloon, his eyes scanned the smoky room for Nancy. Nancy had a slim figure with dainty feet and hands. Nancy's most striking feature was her eyes–they looked almost "doe" like and lovely. On this evening, she wore her emerald green satin gown, for Nancy worked as a saloon girl in the Lady Luck Saloon. A pert bosom pushed against the material of her dress in just the right places.

The two lovers were suddenly interrupted by a man of about thirty-eight years. "That's my girl you're ogling there kid!"

Nancy turned to face Milo Jergens, and when she did, her face turned white as a sheet. She softly and carefully whispered to Mike,

"You'd better go. Milo is a very jealous man, and I've heard he has killed other men before."

"I'm not afraid of him, Mike replied. Tell him to go away."

"I heard you, whelp! Too bad you ain't wearing a gun. I'd call you out and leave your dead carcass for the undertaker!"

Mike rose to his feet, "Take off that gun, Mr. Milo, and I'll fight you with fists, fair and square."

"I've a better idea, Sonny. Go get yourself a gun and I'll teach you some manners."

"I ain't no gunman, Mister," came Mike's answer.

"Well, maybe you'd better become one. Especially, if you think that you can just waltz in here and take my girl," Milo sneered.

Mike Wilkes hung his head for a long moment. After an eternity of seconds, he looked up and straight at Milo's face.

"All right, Milo. I will become a gunman. I will come back here with a gun and I will face you out like you want."

"No, Mike!" cried Nancy. "Don't do it. You might die! You could become just like him!"

"Yah, Sonny. I aim to goad you every day that you come into town. One day, you will be wearing a gun, and that is the day you'll die."

* *

Mike Wilkes tipped his hat to Nancy, strode out of the Lady Luck Saloon, mounted his bay and turned toward the Sumner Ranch.

With Mike gone, Nancy Walters turned to Milo Jergens, "I am not your girl and I never will be! Just because you keep scaring off my friends don't mean that you own me! I will find a way, and then, Milo Jergens, you will never bother me again!"

Milo drew back his hand to strike Nancy, but a stern voice came from behind him, "MILO! You so much as touch that girl and I'll get J.C. Kincaid to throw you in jail."

Jergens turned to face Louise Montrose, owner of the Lady Luck saloon. He stared at Louise with venom in his eyes, "You mind yore own business, Saloon Lady."

"Nancy is my business, Milo. She is one of my girls, and by God, you do her wrong, I'll see you pay for it."

Milo growled back, "Maybe *YOU* ought to be smacked, too. Smart-mouthed women deserve to be beat."

Louise Montrose met Milo's eyes with a stern look of her own as she issued her own challenge to him, "Milo, you sound like you have a big problem. I've heard that you have a wife. Do you beat her like you talk here? Maybe I'll mention that to a lawman and have him ride on out to your farm. Women don't deserve to be beat by the likes of you. If a beating is what you have in mind, then maybe you should be beat by a <u>couple</u> of men."

Milo took a step toward Louise. A voice interrupted them. "Hi, Louise. Is there something wrong?"

Milo turned to face Sheriff J.C. Kincaid. Louise Montrose addressed the lawman, "No, J.C., Milo was just leaving."

Milo glared at Louise, turned on his heel and left the saloon without another word.

Louise turned her head and eyes to the floor, but J.C. wasn't going to let Louise deal alone with whatever bothered her. "Alright, Louise. What is it? I know you and there is something that just don't set right. Tell me what is on your mind."

"All right, J.C., I'll tell you. I've heard that Milo is married, but he is in here every so often. He is rough with girls, especially Nancy. Nancy likes that young wrangler, Mike Wilkes, and they have a special thing going. Milo came in here tonight and challenged Mike Wilkes to a shoot out. Mike never carries a gun, well, except for a rifle. Mike told Milo that he would learn the gun and then come back here for him. Nancy is just out of her mind with fear for Mike."

Louise continued, "J.C., Milo is a trouble maker and a bully. None of the girls like him. The only reason that Nancy tolerates him is that he pays good in tips. She plans to save up her money. Furthermore, I believe that Milo beats his wife and then comes into town and looks to reinforce his power on other folks, especially saloon girls. I wish that you would just ride on out there one day soon and check it out."

Sheriff Kincaid shook his head, "Louise, I can't do that. I've not heard any complaints from the wife, and besides that, I have no jurisdiction on that farm. My authority ends at the city limits."

"Well, then, J.C.," Louise let him know, "I want to speak to Cole Stockton. I know that he has the authority."

"Alright, Louise. I'll speak to Cole about it. Other than that, would you have dinner with me tonight after I make the early rounds?"

"J.C., why do you even have to ask? Just come in here and take me by the hand. Lead me out the door and take me to the Café."

JC grinned his reply, "Louise, do you think I'm nuts? Why, every man in this saloon with a gun would shoot me, especially if you were in the middle of one of those good songs that you sing."

Louise laughed gaily. She knew exactly what J.C. was speaking about. She was the main attraction at the Lady Luck Saloon and more than one rough-appearing man that would likely kill if anything happened to their star song bird.

"All right, J.C. Pick me up at midnight. We'll eat over at Lucy Todd's Café."

J.C. Kincaid smiled widely in appreciation, "Great, Louise! Twelve O'clock, and we'll have a wonderful midnight meal for two. Sure glad she's open all night."

Louise giggled and put her hand to J.C. Kincaid's face.

* *

At the Sumner Ranch, Laura Sumner stood at the main corral with Jud Ellison, Juan Socorro, and Scotty when to their surprise, Mike Wilkes came slowly riding into the LS Ranch yard. He looked like he had a heavy load on his shoulders, and his eyes appeared lost in thought.

When Laura stepped toward Mike, the other two men stuck around to see what was wrong. Laura turned to him, "Mike, you look like you've lost your best friend. Want to talk about it?"

Wilkes looked up into Laura's crystal blue eyes and knew better than to lie. He related the story.

Laura and the wranglers looked at Mike. Jud Ellison turned to Mike and told him straight out, "Well, Mike, were I you, I would talk to the best. I know you think that you have this to do, but speak to Cole Stockton about it. He may just have an alternative for you."

Laura faced Mike and softly said, "I'll speak to Cole about this. Mike, you are no gunman and I, for one, do not want you to become one. I like you just as you are, and if I know your young lady, she doesn't want it either."

"You are right there, Miss Laura. Nancy told me that I would become just like Milo if I took up the gun."

"She is right, Mike. Once you kill with the gun, there is no turning back. Hard men will follow you for no other reason than to kill you because you were considered fast with that gun. They want to be the fastest and most accurate. No, Mike, you don't need that. Let Cole Stockton think this out for you. He knows best. Will you agree to that?"

"Yes, Miss Laura. I know that Mr. Stockton is the best. I will listen to his advice."

* *

Cole Stockton rode onto the LS Ranch and dismounted before the stable. He led Warrior to his stall and began rubbing him down. Presently, Laura Sumner appeared at his side. She smiled, but that smile appeared forced and thoughtful.

"What's on your mind, Laura?" Cole asked.

"Cole, Mike Wilkes has been called out by a two-bit gunny named Milo Jergens. Mike told Jergens that he would learn the gun and meet him. I want you to—well, Cole; I don't really know what I want you to do. I only know that Mike is no gunfighter and that he really needs your help. Will you speak to him?"

"Laura, you know this is the West. If a man gets called out, he is bound to go or be called a coward. That is the unwritten, but understood law of the West. I cannot interfere with that."

Laura held an almost frantic look on her face.

"W-e-l-l, O.K., I can speak with Mike. Perhaps I can guide him a bit."

"Cole, I don't want you to teach him the gun. Mike is a God-fearing nice young man and the gun is not the answer. You know that from your own experiences. If you teach him the gun and he wins this fight, a lot of hardened men will hunt him down. If you don't teach him the gun, he will be branded a coward. That also will play heavy on his mind and I fear what he will do. If he faces that bully without your advice, he will be shot down and probably killed. I don't want that. I want *justice*. Will you do it, Cole?"

Laura continued, "Just as a matter of thought, I've heard stories that Milo beats his wife and then rides into town full of himself. He turns that self-induced power into his own will and mistreats several people—mainly the girls that work in saloons. I have heard through the grapevine that other townsfolk suspect that he might go over the edge and kill again. He killed that young man last year in the street, you remember, and was not convicted because the young man drew first. I don't want that to happen to Mike Wilkes."

"All right, Laura." Cole conceded, "I will look into it."

* *

At first light of the day following, Cole Stockton rode into town and dismounted in front of the jail.

Sheriff J.C. Kincaid looked up from his morning coffee and breakfast. "Morning, Cole. Have some eggs, sausage, and biscuits with me?"

"Of course, J.C. I've never turned down a free breakfast yet. By the way, J.C., what have you heard recently about Milo Jergens?"

"Funny you should ask that, Cole. Louise had a confrontation with Milo Jergens just the other evening. That man is dangerous. I was told that he called Mike Wilkes out and was just about to back slap Nancy when Louise stopped him, and he was steaming up to backslap Louise when I stepped into the situation. Louise asked me to ride on out to his place and check into stories of his wife beating. You know I don't have jurisdiction there. Louise would like you to check into it."

"J.C., this is the second time in twenty-four hours that I've heard that very same thing. You know, I think I <u>will</u> ride on out there. Besides, I want to talk to ole Milo. I want to know just what manner of man he really is. I have promised Laura that I would speak to Mike Wilkes about the situation."

"Cole, you remember last year, the gunfight between Milo and that young drifter?"

"Yes, I do. That shooting was over a young saloon girl, too. Witnesses swore that the young drifter drew first. I can't help that now. I intend that it shall not happen again."

"The man is crazy mean, Cole, mean to the bone when he feels that he is in charge."

"Well, I guess that the key is to not let him be in charge of the situation. Like I said, J.C., I'll ride out there and look around."

* *

Near to just after noon Milo Jergens looked up from his chair next to the door of his ramshackle home and saw the tall lanky rider approaching on the handsome chestnut with blazed face.

His eyes darkened somewhat and his face turned stern. He knew the man riding onto his farm by sight and reputation only, and this man was no one to trifle with. If Milo Jergens thought that he was fast with his gun, that notion dispersed as he watched Cole Stockton ride easily up to within ten feet of him.

"What do you want here, Marshal?"

"Well, Milo, I heard that you were just itching for a gunfight. I thought that I would just ride out here and see for myself just how bad you wanted one."

"Are you trying to scare me, Marshal? Are you threatening me?"

"No, Milo. Just curious on why you picked on Mike Wilkes for a gunfight. I suppose that you think the kid is going to be easy pickings, huh? Well, never mind that for the moment—I want to see your wife out here and speak with her for a moment. Some people in town think that you are a wife beater and I've been asked to check up on it. I don't cotton much to that kind of behavior."

"A man's wife is his own business, Marshal. She ain't coming out here."

"Oh, yes, she will, Milo. I am responsible for the safety of all citizens in the Lower Colorado and I'm making it my business. Call her out here."

"All right, Marshal. Woman! Get on out here. The Marshal wants to see and speak with you!"

Cole Stockton waited a long moment and finally Elsa Jergens stepped slowly through the door. She acted afraid and kept her head down. She was a slight woman with long brown hair and eyes, her dress, shapeless and stained simple gingham, was the dress of most farm bred women in the territory. She trembled slightly as she stood in front of the door.

"Mrs. Jergens, are you all right?"

"Yes, Marshal. I am fine." Elsa's eyes; however, told a different story. They looked pleading in nature, and the dark circles around them made them sink into her face.

U.S. Marshal Cole Stockton smiled at her and with a soft voice said, "All right, Mrs. Jergens, I'm sorry to bother you."

Elsa Jergens turned silently and went back into the house.

Milo was quick to speak up, "See, Marshal. There ain't nothing wrong here. Them folks lied."

"Well, Milo, maybe they did and maybe they didn't. I'll say this—I might just decide to ride on out here every so often and water my horse at your trough. Should I find something out of the ordinary, I will take a closer look and you won't like it. Now, back to Mike Wilkes. It seems to me, that a man that has a wife shouldn't be calling young men out in the street for a gunfight over saloon girls. Care to comment on that, Milo?"

"You just mind your own business, Marshal."

"Shootings are my business, Milo. As a matter of fact, I'm going to have a long talk with Mike Wilkes. I am going to give him some good advice and I think that he will heed it. Yah, Milo, come on in to town in a couple of days—and bring your gun with you."

Cole Stockton had that silly grin on his face as he slowly backed Warrior up a few yards, then turned and trotted off the Jergens farm.

Milo closed his eyes for a long moment and thought, "Cole Stockton is speaking with Mike Wilkes. I'll bet that he is teaching him some kind of gunfighter tricks. Well, no matter. Mike Wilkes can't possibly learn that fast—not in two days."

* *

Cole sat easy in saddle as he rode away from Milo's farm. Suddenly he smiled to himself. Then, he began to whistle a merry tune. He chuckled loudly with the flash of mischief that crossed his mind. The solution to Milo and the impending gunfight with Mike Wilkes became vivid to him. If Milo wanted a gunfight, he would get his gunfight.

CHAPTER ELEVEN

A Helping Hand

Mike Wilkes sat on his bed in the bunkhouse holding his head in his hands. He thought, "Oh, God, I've done it now. There is no way that I can best <u>anyone</u> in a gunfight. I am going to be killed. What would Mother do? What would Nancy do?"

Just then, the door to the bunkhouse opened and Cole Stockton stepped inside and up to him.

"Mike, I heard that you accepted Milo Jergens' challenge for a gunfight. Laura asked me to speak with you."

"Yessir, Marshal Stockton. I just wish that I could take it all back. I dearly love Nancy, but there is no way that I can face Milo with a gun."

"Well, Mike. When a man is called out, he has to go. That's the unwritten law of the West. I believe, however, that I can help you, without you actually having to draw that gun."

"Marshal Stockton, I shore wish that you could, but—but, Milo intends to draw his."

"Yes, Mike—I know that. You will just have to trust me. Will you do that?"

"Yes, Marshal. I trust you—I trust you with my life."

"Good. Now, there are some mighty good things at that supper table. Go and get some. Don't worry no more. I will speak with you more late in the evening tomorrow."

Stockton turned with a grin on his face and left the bunkhouse.

Mike Wilkes began to feel better about himself and his situation. Rising, he went to supper with the other wranglers. Mike felt so good that he ate up two full plates of sliced beef, boiled potatoes, and string beans—all along with near to six fresh biscuits sopping in fresh butter and dripping with honey.

* *

Laura Sumner watched silently as Cole Stockton ate up two plates of beef, potatoes, string beans, and drank three cups of freshly brewed coffee. She couldn't understand it, he held that silly grin on his face and seemed to be silently plotting some mysterious shenanigan once again.

Laura asked him straight out, "Cole, did you talk with Mike?"

"Yes, Laura, I did."

"Well?"

"Well, what?"

"Well, what did you tell him?"

"Mike will meet with Milo in the street about two days from now. I will make sure of that and both will be wearing guns."

"Cole Stockton! I asked you not to teach Mike the gun."

"I didn't."

"You didn't teach him the gun? Are you crazy, Cole? That bully Milo will just shoot him down like he did that young drifter last year."

"No, Laura, I don't think that he will."

"How can you say that, Cole? Do you know something that you aren't telling me?"

"Yes. You might say that."

Laura Sumner looked directly into those blue-green eyes and asked, "Do you want to tell me?"

"No. As a matter of fact, I haven't ironed out all the details yet. I won't tell you until I do."

"Cole! This is Laura. Mike is one of my very best wranglers, and one of the most wel-liked young men in town. I won't stand by and let him be simply shot down by the likes of Milo. I will take all my wranglers into town and shoot that SOB myself before Mike Wilkes gets gunned down by the likes of him."

"Well, Laura. You do what you want to do. The solution, however, is evident to me."

"Cole, you aren't making any sense."

"Oh, yes, I am. You just don't see it yet."

* *

Two days later in the Jergens cabin, an enraged man screamed, "Woman! This is the worst breakfast I ever seen. This is garbage!"

Milo Jergens suddenly jumped up from his table and grabbing up his plate threw it at his wife, Elsa. She ducked and the plate and all the food on it smacked into the wall behind her.

Milo strode quickly to her and grabbed her roughly by her hair. He dragged her across the room, her screams falling on empty ears.

He then dragged her to her feet and smacked her straight in the face with a meaty fist. He smashed his fist into her stomach. Elsa Jergens slammed to the floor like she was hit with a ten-ton hammer.

Milo picked her up and then rammed her head first into the nearest wall. She passed out and Milo grinned.

To his crazed mind, he was full of power. He would now go into town and meet with that young Mike Wilkes. He was thirsty for blood and more power. Today, he would kill again, just like he killed that young drover a year ago.

Milo remembered it vividly. The young drover was no match for him and it pleased him that he held the power over life and death. It thrilled him to watch the drover die at his hand.

Today, another would die at his hand and he would once again hold the immaculate power in his mind. He was invincible and best of all—no lawman in his right mind would interfere. This was the "Law of the West" and once challenged, a man was committed to answer it.

Yes, today, Milo would once again prove his manhood to all those present in town. He was not a simple farmer like they thought. He, Milo Jergens, was a man who held a life and death decision at his very fingertips—the grips of his Colt.

Milo looked down upon his still unconscious wife and thought,

"Yah, and when I get home. If my supper is not what I want, I'll beat you more."

Jergens went to the peg holding his gunbelt and strapped it on. He opened the loading gate of his revolver and slipped in a sixth cartridge. He leered a crooked smile.

He strode to his small stable and saddled up his favorite horse, Reaper, a dark brown, almost black, with a single white diamond on his forehead. This was the same horse that Milo rode when he killed that young man a year ago, and he considered it his death horse.

Milo mounted and rode slowly toward Miller's Station, the small town near the passes.

* *

U.S. Marshal Cole Stockton rode slowly onto the Jergens farm and eased Warrior up to the water trough. All was silent. He dismounted and let the reins drop to the ground. Warrior moved slowly to the water trough and began to drink.

Something was amiss. Milo didn't seem to be home.

Suddenly, from inside the cabin came a loud shriek of pain.

Stockton dashed to the door of the Jergens homestead with Colt drawn and kicked the door open.

He found Elsa Jergens lying on the floor holding her stomach, with tears of pain in her eyes.

"Elsa, what is wrong and how can I help you?"

"He beat me, Marshal. God, he beat me. I am with child! I fear that he has killed my baby! He's beaten me and now I'm losing this child! It's not time, it's too early. God, it hurts."

Cole Stockton bent down to Elsa and gently picked her up. He carried her to her bed and laid her down.

"Mrs. Jergens, I need to examine you. Will you let me?"

"Yes, Marshal. Oh, God the pain!"

Cole Stockton drew off the woman's underthings.

"Holy God," thought Cole to himself. "This woman is having a baby, and it is coming <u>now</u>!"

Cole withdrew his Colt placing it close to hand on the bed and took off his gunbelt. He placed the leather into the woman's mouth and told her to bite down hard. She did, and then, his ears rang with the scream as a blood encased, deceased, unborn child slowly emitted from the woman into his hands.

Cole Stockton gritted his teeth and swore loudly.

* *

Milo Jergens rode into Miller's Station and tied up at the hitching rack in front of the Lady Luck Saloon. He grinned widely. Mike Wilkes had been told to be here at noon. He was going to once again exert power.

* *

Mike Wilkes saddled his bay gelding. He spoke soft and soothingly to it. He wore a borrowed gunbelt. He wore it in the fashion that Cole Stockton advised him to wear it, and it felt extremely uncomfortable to him.

"Well, Abe, it looks a lot like this will be our last ride together. I want you to know that I love you. You are a great horse." Mike's eyes filled with tears.

Mike led his bay out of the stable area and was immediately surprised.

Mounted and lined up in front of him were all the wranglers of the Sumner Horse Ranch. Laura Sumner was with them.

Laura looked Mike Wilkes straight in the eye and said, "Mike. You don't have to do this."

"Oh, yes I do, Miss Sumner. I have been called out and I must go or be branded a coward for the rest of my life."

"Then, we're all going, too, Mike." Laura spoke with determination. The entire Sumner Ranch followed Mike Wilkes into town, tied up their horses along the street and looked silently up the street toward the Lady Luck Saloon.

At twenty minutes til noon, Milo Jergens planned to step through the batwing doors of the Lady Luck and stand in the middle of the street.

Following tradition, Mike Wilkes would step into the center of the street and they would walk the forty steps each to face each other about twenty yards apart. They would appraise each other, and then--then, hands would reach for guns and one would die.

The minutes ticked slowly, and Laura saw beads of sweat form on Mike Wilkes' forehead. She stepped up to Mike and softly spoke into his ear, "Mike, you don't have to do this."

Shaking his head, Mike Wilkes brushed Laura aside, and with a deep breath, stepped out into the dusty street. He stood there alone. Mike Wilkes recalled vividly the instructions from Cole Stockton.

"Mike. Walk slowly into the center of the street. Turn and face him. Look straight into the man's eyes and never flinch. Look him straight into the eyes and think to yourself—I am going to be shot and I will endure the pain. I am a strong person. I will live through this. One other thing, Mike—trust in the Almighty. He knows best."

Mike Wilkes reached down and touched the Colt in his holster. He eased it out and then, let it slip silently, naturally back into the leather sheath.

He softly grinned to himself. He had done all that Cole Stockton told him to do. He took a long deep breath and faced toward the Lady Luck. He swallowed hard as Milo Jergens slipped out of the batwings, and moved to the center of the dirt street. Milo held a vicious look about him.

The two men stared at each other across the one hundred yard distance. Milo started his "gunman's walk" toward Mike. Suddenly, Miller's Station Townspeople began to filter out to the street in groups of two and three or even four at a time. They lined the boardwalks of the town and silently watched.

Mike Wilkes thought, "Look at this. The entire town is turned out for my death."

Milo Jergens thought, "Look at this. The entire town is turned out to see me kill this young man. I'll be talked about and I'll be seen as a real gunfighter, not a simple-minded farmer."

The distance closed and suddenly they stood not more than thirty yards apart.

Milo glared at his quarry. "I see you're wearing a gun. That's good because I am going to draw and shoot you dead."

Mike Wilkes suddenly grinned at Milo, "I think not, *farmer*! I hope you've said your prayers' cause if you even tickle that hogleg, I'm going to shoot you."

Jergens balked for a moment. Where did this yelp of a man get a spine?

His mind flashed back to his meeting with Cole Stockton and the thought once again crossed his mind, "Stockton has spoke with that young wrangler and taught him some *tricks*."

Then, Milo thought once again. "Yeah, tricks. That's it. Tricks to try and confuse me. This is a trick to try and confuse me. The kid is a dead man. I am going to draw and shoot him dead."

Milo's hand moved closer to his gun.

Over three dozen "clicks" of metal sliding against metal met Milo's ears. His eyes suddenly turned to the crowd along the boardwalk. Each person, man or woman, standing along the walk had a firearm in their hand and had cocked the hammer back. They were waiting. Waiting for what?

At the same time, Mike Wilkes was suddenly joined by Laura Sumner and all ten of her wranglers. The wranglers held Winchester rifles at the ready along with grim and determined faces.

Milo Jergens looked with stunned surprise at the townspeople that lined the boardwalks of the town.

Each citizen held a rifle, shotgun or pistol, and all were cocked and leveled directly at Milo Jergens.

Milo inhaled sharply. This development was not going as planned. He should be the hero of the hour. He would be the man that shot down yet another victim of his gun and those that witnessed the action would call him "gunfighter."

Milo hesitated and thought, "What will happen if I touch my gun? The answer was obvious. Everyone with a gun in their hands would shoot Milo Jergens."

Milo just stood there in front of Mike Wilkes. He didn't know what to do.

Just at that time a slow-moving ranch wagon entered town and the driver eased up to the hitching post in front of Doctor Simmon's office. The driver stepped down from the wagon and surveyed the scene.

Cole Stockton walked directly to the center of the street and touched Mile Wilkes gently on the shoulder.

"Mike, move to your friends. I have business with Milo and my business is urgent. I am sorry, Mike, but you will have to wait your turn."

Mike Wilkes was dumbfounded. He was being gently pushed out of the scene by U.S. Marshal Cole Stockton. Mike did as told and now Milo stood in the center of the street facing the man sometimes referred to as the Angel of Death in certain circles."

Milo Jergens became further dumbfounded. He saw Cole Stockton walk somberly up to Mike Wilkes and softly tell him something. Milo watched incredulously as Cole Stockton replaced Mike Wilkes in the street and stood in front of him to announce, "Milo Jergens, you are under arrest for murder. You have just five seconds to drop your weapon before I kill you."

All eyes now turned toward Milo.

"I have not even drawed my gun against this man yet, Marshal. How can you say anything about murder?"

"Jergens, your wife died in my arms a little over two hours ago. Before she died she delivered a dead child into my own hands. On her death bed she told me of the beatings, and now--you wanted a gunfight, you have one. Touch that gun Milo, cause I want to inflict pain in your body. I want to shoot you to rag dolls, Milo. I want you to feel the burning of hot lead deep within your body as I rob you of your miserable life."

The entire town kept silent, awestruck with the scene before them.

Laura Sumner moved toward Cole Stockton and was motioned back. She knew immediately what that meant. Cole was madder than hell. He was going to kill this man, Milo Jergens, and no one person alive could dissuade him.

Laura spoke softly to Cole, "Cole, you are the law. You can't take this man's life just like that. He must be tried in a court of law for his crimes."

Cole never flinched from Jergens' eyes. He motioned Laura away once again. Laura turned and stepped back to the boardwalk. She hung her head silently and whispered to herself, "I tried. Lord knows, I tried."

"Come on Milo. You think yourself a gunfighter. Prove it—draw your gun against me."

Milo stood dumfounded for a long moment. He came to town to kill a young man known as Mike Wilkes. Suddenly, the entire town seemed to want to kill him. Now, he was facing U.S. Marshal Cole Stockton for a gunfight. This was not going his way. Furthermore, Cole Stockton issued him the challenge.

To not meet Stockton in the street would brand him a coward for all to see. Secondly, Stockton now told him that he was under arrest for Elsa's murder. He had never wanted the baby. Stockton ordered him to throw down his gun.

Milo Jergens looked straight into Stockon's eyes and he saw the fires of Hell. His right hand swept toward the weapon in his holster. He saw no other way. He had to kill Cole Stockton in order to survive.

Milo's Colt rose from his holster, and suddenly, he looked wide eyed and screamed, "No!"

Cole Stockton's Colt was already centered on him. Suddenly— smoke, fire, and then hot lead spun directly into the center of Milo's body. He jerked violently with each ugly thud of heavy .45 caliber lead.

Three bullets hit Milo Jergens in succession. He immediately slammed to the ground holding his midsection and screaming for a Doctor.

Stockton walked cautiously up to Milo and placed the bore of his Colt against Milo's forehead. He cocked the hammer back, and then spoke softly, "You are damned lucky that I'm wearing this star, Milo. For two cents I'd end your life right here and now. But, you'll live to stand trial in Judge Wilkerson's court. I want to watch you hang for the murder of both your wife and your unborn child."

Stockton suddenly kicked Milo's revolver out of the way, and then motioned for men to carry Milo to Doctor Simmons office.

Sheriff J.C. Kincaid stepped up to Cole. "I'll take it from here, Cole. I think that there are some people who are glad to see you."

Cole turned to look directly into Laura Sumner's crystal blue eyes. She silently mouthed the words, "Thank you."

He smiled at her with that silly grin and then walked right up to her. Their arms slipped around each other and held each other tightly. Laura whispered into his ear, "Just how did you know that the entire town would turn on Milo?"

He whispered back, "W-e-l-l, you said it yourself. Mike Wilkes is a well-liked young man in this town. That cowboy last year was a drifter, not known to anyone. I figured that the townspeople had had just about enough of Milo and that they weren't going to let him bully Mike. Besides, you said yourself that you were going to bring all your boys into town and shoot that SOB if he harmed even one hair on Mike's head. Now, with that kind of backing, I just naturally spoke a few words here and there to set people's minds to thinking. I'm glad my message got through. I didn't have to teach Mike the gun and he didn't have to pull that Colt. Speaking of Mike—where is he?"

Cole and Laura parted for an instant and looked around.

Mike Wilkes was lying sprawled in the dirt street. A very excited young Nancy was on top of him, smothering him with kisses.

The townspeople mostly held grins and smiles on their faces as they turned and went about their business. Cole and Laura turned to each other once again. Their arms went around each other and the kiss that followed could have started a raging prairie fire.

Chapter Twelve

Riding the Circuit

In late November, Ole Man Winter had a tight grip on the Rocky Mountain areas.

My bound duty required me to ride the cold and windy trails and see to the welfare of all of the Southern Colorado residents. Most knew me by now, and for the better part, I'd be invited in for coffee and various meals that just happened to be on the stove. Not that I minded much——trail jerky and cold biscuits just didn't cut it when a man could savor the aroma of bacon and eggs frying, meat roasting in the oven, and best of all—the unmistakable smell of fresh bread right out of the oven.

There were others, though, that didn't particularly care to meet up with me, but a man in my profession eventually meets all.

I am Cole Stockton, United States Marshal.

* *

I had found in the past that most of the larger ranches had taken care of their own during the intense cold of the winter months and things their way were relatively quiet.

There were the usual losses of weak stock to the wolves and other scavengers—nature goes on.

My main concerns were those less fortunate, and I wanted to lend a helping hand where needed: kind of a Good Neighbor policy endorsed by the Marshal's office and the Territorial Governor.

During these trips, I also exchanged information with all whom I made contact. People, even ones far from town, had information that might come I handy to a U.S. Marshal.

Folks appraised me of new arrivals in the territory as well as those that had given up and returned to a less wild society.

New arrivals interested me the most. Colorado in these times seemed a most likely hide-a-way for those on the run from something bigger.

There were also those folks that you could possibly refer to as VIP's—meaning *Very Intriguing People*.

One such person was a feller that I met in a saloon in Cripple Creek one time.

He was a dentist named John H. Holliday. Most people just called him "Doc." He was a tall, dark and dashing figure as I recall. Though quite gentlemanly, he possessed deadly skill with a six-gun.

I read much later in newspapers, that Doc joined up with the likes of Wyatt Earp and his clan down in Tombstone, Arizona. News accounts of that association and the ensuing feuds between the Earp's, Holliday, and the McLaurey-Clanton faction plagued the headlines for several months.

I never met Marshal Earp, nor any of his brothers, but someone once told me that if ever we should meet, it would be a sight to see.

There were others, less notable, but equally as lethal, that sought out refuge within the wilds of the Lower Colorado.

Cletus Jackson was one of these men. He was described as a B-I-G man—all muscle. Some even said that his upper arms were as big as an average man's thighs.

I couldn't say that for sure, but I could say without reservation that he was a most powerful man. He was well built physically and deadly with either pistol or rifle.

His favorite weapon, however, was a long, razor-sharp, knife. Stories told that he dearly loved to cut a man's throat just to watch him choke and bleed to death.

As a man on the run from the law, some said that he made his way to the Rockies to escape hanging in the lower lands of Arkansas.

Either way, I had a wanted poster on him for murder, and word was strong that he was definitely in the mountains of Colorado.

* *

On the third day out that I came upon a small cabin with makeshift lean-to stable and corral. A couple of crowbait horses and fairly thin-looking cattle stood penned in the corral.

It was about as poor an outfit that I ever saw. I hailed the house. A few moments later, a tall thin-looking gent and a wisp of a girl came to the door.

I introduced myself, and they appeared quite nervous about me being there. Finally, they explained that they had come upon this cabin, found it deserted, and sort of took up homesteading it.

I knew about this small farm and advised them that the previous owners, rather, the previous occupants had given up the frontier and had taken the road back to civilization.

They seemed to settle down after that, and told me their names— Jon and Carol Simon.

I also advised them that all they had to do was to get to the nearest land office and file a claim on it. Then, it would be theirs for as long as they wanted to work it.

They invited me in for some coffee, and I gladly accepted. We talked some over that coffee, and they told me they had been married in Tennessee, and traveled north to Colorado in order to start a new life for themselves.

This was a common story, folks wanting to build something of their own life in a new territory. They were people to grow with the land.

I decided to see if the nearest rancher could stake this young couple for a season whilst they got on their feet. Meanwhile, these folks needed meat. I thought I might track down a deer for them. I had seen some deer tracks back a ways and told them that I would be back within a few hours or so. They appreciated my offer.

* *

Warrior and I cut the deer trail and began to follow it. A few hours later, we came upon a bloody scene. The carcass of a mule ear deer lay bleeding and cut up.

The animal had been shot with a heavy bore rifle, and only the best parts of the meat seemed to have been hastily taken. The rest was left to the scavengers. Now, who in his right mind would do such a thing?

I carefully checked the scene and judging by the tracks left, a very large man had done this. My mind immediately thought of Cletus Jackson.

By the looks of it, it could be him—or, might not. This situation stood for a much closer examination. If it were Cletus, he would be within the vicinity, and those folks at the small farm were in a lot of danger.

I wrapped up a good bit of the best remaining parts of the venison and rode back toward the cabin. I wanted to get there fast and warn the couple of the possible "visitor."

Then, I would get back to pick up the trail and start tracking this feller down before sundown.

Those folks seemed mighty thankful for the meat, and by the looks on their faces, they hadn't had a decent meat meal in quite a while.

They invited me to share a stew with them, but I declined, taking a vow to stop back in for a meal as soon as I found this person I intended to hunt.

* *

Tracking back to the deer kill, I began thinking about Laura. We had been through quite a bit together lately, and she stood out in my mind as a woman to "ride the river" with.

Folks around her neck of the woods kind of smiled at us whenever they saw us together. I thought that I caught some "knowing" glances every so often, especially from the womenfolk in town. Now, I thought I'd seen them very same "glances" from buzzards perched up high waiting on a piece of meat.

The older ladies certainly seemed that they would wait for the day that we would announce our intentions to the world. To tell the truth, I'd been thinking about it more and more lately. Perhaps, when I got back from this dutiful ride.

My daydreaming came to an abrupt halt with the whistling of a heavy bore piece of lead sailing past my right shoulder.

The rifle report sounded a split second later.

I jerked my Winchester out of the boot as I hastily dismounted and yelled at Warrior to "get the hell out of here."

I dived behind some fallen logs just as splinters flew up. Again, the rifle report sounded.

This guy was higher up and had me in his sights.

"Cole Stockton," I said to myself, "you have gotten yourself in a real mess this time."

I chanced a quick peek around the edge of the log pile, fully expecting to get another round thrown at me. Silence prevailed.

Somebody intended to play around with me and I didn't like it much. I eased up and looked straight up the snow-scattered slope. No rifle shots rang out, no lead came singing my way. I took a deep breath and stood up.

Nothing but silence greeted my ears, and an icy cold wind sighing through the pines stung my cheeks.

Warrior had been taught to stay within calling distance, and I knew that he was out there. I called him and he came trotting right up to me.

Together we walked up the slope toward the spot where that lead had come flying down. I found it. Yep! Someone had waited here——a big man by the looks of the indentation in the dirt and snow.

Three .56 caliber casings lay where he had been. His tracks led to a horse, and now he was gone.

I mounted Warrior and we once again began following this hombre. I would be a lot more careful this time——looking for ambush places before I rode into them.

I sure wished that I knew for certain just who this person was. It would help to know that it was indeed Cletus Jackson that I was trailing.

* *

The tracks led upward toward the rocky crests, and I began to grow quite leery of this trail. I figured this person wanted me to follow him up past the tree line into the rocks.

Well, two could play at this game, and I veered immediately to the right. I rode for half an hour, then turned upward again——angling left. With luck, I would come right up behind him—unless, of course, he turned left. Then, I would be further behind him. Well, that's the chance I took.

Darkness overtook us and I had to stop for a cold camp to wait out the dark night. I could light no fire for I didn't want to advertise my position. At the same time, he could light no fire because I would see it and find him.

I bundled up in my heavy coat and ate a chaw of cold beef jerky with cold trail biscuit, while my mind began conjuring up a large thick slab of beefsteak broiling over Laura's cook stove.

I could almost taste her thick flaky biscuits and berry jam. The thing that gnawed at me the most, though, was the coffee. I surely loved a good dark cup of coffee. I let out a long sigh, and continued to chew my tough jerky. I closed my eyes and fell into a light sleep, my Colt revolver close at hand.

* *

I woke up before the early gray of dawn and stomped feeling back into my toes. The high country is extremely cold at night, and the wind chills to the bone.

I was in the saddle with first light, and moving as silently as Warrior and I could. We had gone but a few miles when his ears pricked up. I looked intently in the direction that he was looking, and then, I saw him. He was crouched down behind a large rock. His back was to us and he was watching the downwind trail.

He was a big man——perhaps the largest I had ever seen, and he held what appeared to be a Sharps rifle.

I shucked my Winchester, and letting the reins trail hitch, I moved forward and closer to him as quietly as I could.

I was about thirty yards from him when he sensed that I was coming up on him. He turned to face me and started to lift that rifle when I issued the challenge, "U.S. Marshal. Drop that gun and grab sky!"

"Howdy, Marshal! Been waiting fer ya. I knowed you was on my backtrail and I can't let you take me back——not alive anyways. You are going to have to kill me first."

And with that, he leveled that rifle straight at me. That's when I shot him.

Three times I worked that lever, and three times my Winchester fired molten lead into this man. He dropped his rifle and began running toward me. A long sharp hunting knife was in his right hand. I couldn't believe my eyes.

"Damn," I cursed under my breath, and drew my Colt.

I stood there, him charging right at me, and aimed straight at his middle. I hit him solidly three more times at fairly close range before he staggered and stumbled to breathlessly lie heaped on the ground—— two yards from my still smoking and once again cocked revolver.

I walked cautiously to him and kicked the knife away.

I pointed the Colt straight at his face and looking into his pain-wretched eyes told him, "You give me any more reason, I'll leave your dead carcass for the vultures."

He moaned painfully, and I produced a set of handcuffs. It wasn't until I had him searched and cuffed, that I checked his wounds.

Any normal man would be dead by now. But, this feller was wore a heavy coat and had so much muscle around his chest and middle that my bullets had imbedded in him——not substantially hitting any vital organs that I could tell. He was bleeding some, but not too badly.

The plan form in my mind. I would rig a sturdy travois, and drag him back to that settler cabin. I sure didn't want to try and help him up on a horse, as he outweighed me by about a hundred pounds, and all of those pounds, muscle.

I took that knife of his and cut some saplings for a travois, lashed them together with some rawhide cut from his own coat, and tied the poles to his stirrups.

"Get up into it!" I commanded.

"Make me!" he retorted.

"O.K.," I replied, "either get onto the travois, or I'll put a rope around your thick neck and drag your carcass down the mountain."

I must've sounded sincere about it because he groaned and moaned his way onto that skid, and got ready for a jolting ride downhill.

About four hours later, we pulled up in front of the settler cabin. I dismounted and stood over my wounded giant. "Mind your manners and I'll get you tended to. Cause any trouble and I'll shoot you point blank dead."

I called out to the folks inside.

The door opened only a crack at first. Then, slowly widened. The couple moved outside, and said, "Marshal Stockton, we are sure glad to see you. There has been someone skulking around our cabin at night since you left, and we have been afraid to venture outside. Whatever it was killed our stock——slit their throats in the night. We found some big footprints in the corral and leanto. There have been strange scraping noises in the night, but we did not open the door. We just sat there with our shotgun ready."

I turned to the big man. "You do this, too——Cletus?"

He looked up at me and said, "Cletus? No, my name is not Cletus! Name's Lem——Lem Dugan! I thought that you were after me for killing that rancher's steer last month during the blizzard. I thought that you would hang me for that steer. I heard tell that folks were hung for taking a man's cattle, even for food when your family was starving. That's why I run away, and made you follow me."

I looked down at Lem Dugan and sighed. I reached down and to his surprise took the cuffs off him.

"Ma'am? Could you look after his wounds? I will take a look around."

The Simons helped Lem into the cabin where they extracted the lead and patched him up.

I closely surveyed the surrounding area. There were indeed big footprints——just about as big as Lem's, and as deep. No shotgun was going to stop this man. That's when I thought of Lem's rifle——a Sharps .56——a buffalo gun.

* *

Darkness fell, and I waited outside in the corner of the leanto shed——that Sharps .56 in my hand.

I found myself on another icy cold night in the elements, well, I thought, that was why they paid me fifty dollars a month, food, found, and all the bullets I could shoot.

I settled down and gnawed on some more of that trail jerky. Warrior rested in one of the stalls, and we waited. At around midnight, I heard it——an eerie scraping sound.

My eyes searched the darkness along the cabin.

Suddenly, there was a slight movement. A large hulk moved along the cabin wall and the moonlight glinted on a long silver object. A long knife?

I raised up that Sharps, lined up on the hulk, and challenged, "Cletus! Damn you——drop that knife and raise your hands!"

Only a scuffle of feet sounded as he rushed toward me, that knife raised for a strike.

I shot him straight in the middle, the weapon resounding with a loud heavy boom.

The hulk staggered backward. I quickly reloaded the single shot weapon and lined up another shot. He came again, and I shot him again. It only slowed him down.

I once again reloaded quickly and when he was close enough for me to see the ugly of his twisted and hatred-wrenched face, I shot him again——right in the chest.

He slammed backward and fell lifelessly to the icy cold ground.

I reloaded and approached him very cautiously. The folks inside called out to me, and I yelled to them to bring a lantern.

The light from the lantern confirmed finally that Cletus Jackson was indeed here in Colorado—his lifeless body lying at my feet with three .56 caliber slugs in his chest.

* *

The next morning, between three of us, I got Cletus' body loaded on the travois, had that bowl of hot stew with the Simons couple and told Lem that I would take care of his "debt" to the rancher feller. He actually invited me to drop in at his cabin, almost thirty miles further north, and to meet his family. I promised that I would, the next ride on the circuit.

I dropped by some of the larger ranches on the way to Judge Wilkerson's with Cletus' body and explained the situation about the Simons and Lem. They told me that the ranchers would watch out for them as well as their own.

Nature has a way of watching out for its own, and so should folks, especially, for them that want to build a new life. Sometimes, all it takes is a helping hand, and one will find a lot of good neighbors.

Facing southward once again, I could almost taste that steak and coffee on Laura's cook stove.

CHAPTER THIRTEEN

Doc Simmons

I'd heard it said by many a citizen in the wilds that the lawman finally brought civilization to the West. I reflected on that many a time. Being a lawman myself, I had a lot of time to think on such things. I did my thinking while out on lonely trails searching for those that done wrong to someone.

I came to the conclusion that if any one person was significant to the West, it was a man of medicine: the doctor.

Some folks sought out his cures for ailing and old age. Others sought him out to make it easier on child bearing. Whatever the ailment, the doctor knew pretty much how to handle it.

Then, again, there were those that sought his services for a more deadly or, shall I say, for a more life-giving outlook.

Even wounded outlaws cried out for the man of medicine: the one man that they knew could save their miserable lives. I ought to know. I've put lead into many a man and have also taken lead myself when the chips were down.

I have a great respect for a man who would spend many years learning the books as well as the wherefores and whyfores of medicine. His is a skilled art, and many times, he has not received the good words that get often praised to others.

Many times, I saw that people had need of his services, but had little to pay. The doc took whatever they could afford and told them that he would carry their note for as long as they needed to. I guess it fell to that oath that he took when he accepted the job. That oath read something like he was duty bound to help those in need of medical attention whether he received payment or not. Now, that is what I call a dedicated man.

A doctor's services were continually sought out by many, but his payment was rarely equal to his skills. I guess that's why most saloons and general stores usually gave him a discount, or sometimes even just tore up his bill.

The doc even performed services for the Marshal's office. For this, I was allowed to pay him a modest fee of about half of what his services were worth. Somehow, he accepted it with a smile.

I guess when you come right down to it, there were two kinds of people that a true Westerner just didn't want to do harm to. It could get a man hanged in a very short minute. The first were women. The population of women in the West was mighty short, and them that had a good woman were justly thankful of it. The other protected group was the doctor. If a man was known for killing women or a doctor, folks would just naturally trail him down, put a fair amount of lead into him, then hang him for all to see.

Being of some experience, I've often sought out the doctor myself, either to take the lead out and patch me up or to take the lead out've someone I shot myself. That's my job, Cole Stockton, United States Marshal, Territory of the Lower Colorado.

* *

Around the time of the great annual southern migration, everyone could hear the call of the wild Canadian geese as they winged their way toward the south. Flock after flock could be seen in "V" shaped wedges as they rode the currents of cool October air.

Some flocks would veer from their path momentarily, only to circle several times seemingly to renew their bearings, and then stream forward toward the warm summer days of unknown places to the south of the world.

Doctor Carlin J. Simmons, educated in one of the finest medical schools of the East, served his internship under the most grueling of circumstances: as a battlefield surgeon during the great War Between the States.

He experienced pestilence, carnage, maiming, malnutrition, starvation, gangrene, malaria, small pox, chicken pox, birthing, venereal diseases, and dismemberment.

During the battle of Gettysburg, he worked fervently to save soldiers of both sides from death only to have over fifty percent die from shock, the shock of having limbs removed with very little pain-killing medicine. He worked from one man to another until out of sheer exhaustion, he crumbled to his knees and passed out. Orderlies gently picked him up and carried him to his tent and laid him to rest. Other surgeons experienced likewise.

At the end of the war, Doctor Simmons opened an office in the East. His clientele mainly consisted of women having babies, and an occasional bout of stomach flu.

Although the money was good, he felt restless. He hadn't married yet, and his parents had died during the War.

One day, in his newspaper he saw an advertisement touting opportunities in the West. One of the occupations most requested was that of doctor. A story accompanying the ad explained the opportunities for physicians who moved West to offer their services.

Carlin Simmons laid awake most of the night thinking about that newspaper, and in the morning, he took down his shingle, packed his bags and traveled to St. Louis, Missouri——the jumping off point to the wild and untamed West.

He wandered from town to town administering his medical trade to those in need, and finally, ten years later he arrived in the small town of Miller's Station near the passes between New Mexico and the wilds of the Lower Colorado.

* *

Presently, Doc Simmons walked slowly down the wooden boardwalk toward his upstairs office and clinic he had established. He heard the "honking" of the wild geese and looked skyward. He shook his head affirmatively and muttered to himself, "Well, it looks to be a cold, cold winter coming on. The geese are running early this year."

Doc Simmons turned and walked to the outside stair that led to his office. Upon opening the door and entering his office, the metallic click of a pistol being cocked caught his immediate attention.

Doc Simmons looked quickly to the right. Two men were in his office. One sat lazily on the examination table, his grimy hands toying with the revolver in his hands. The other sat in the doctor's own chair, a hard look in his eyes, and cocked revolver in his hand.

"What do you men want? How did you get in here?"

"We want YOU, Doc. Get your bag and as many medical supplies as you need to patch up five gunshot men. You're coming with us straight away. You cry out, or try to escape, I'll shoot you down and drag your wounded body with us anyway. There's hosses outside for the three of us. Hurry now and no funny business. There's men who will die without your help."

"Alright, I'll go with you. Who are these men? You said that there are five?"

"Yah, Doc, two of them are my brothers, the other three are no account cousins. They die, you die. Get it?"

"Yes. I get it. You boys are the ones that the posse from Fort Collins is looking for. I heard that when you ran out of the bank, that you left two more of your kin lying in the street up there. I also heard that you killed two innocent women and a child on the streets as you shot your way out of town. I heard that twelve of you got away and that possibly five of you were wounded."

The harder looking man in Doc's chair had dressed in rumpled clothes. His hair fell to his shoulders and he sported two tied-down holsters. The grimy-looking man grinned with an evil look, as he jumped from the examination table to the floor. He wore buckskin pants tucked into knee high moccasins and a faded red flannel shirt. He also wore a large Bowie Knife on his gun belt.

"Can I have your names?" asked Doctor Simmons.

"Don't matter none now, Doc. They call me Harley. This here is Cooley, and he just don't trust no doctors."

Doc Simmons reflected on the names.

Harley Judson, and Cooley Blaine. Cooley had a reputation for killing without remorse. His favorite weapon was the knife. He enjoyed cutting on his victims before he mercilessly murdered them.

Harley was also a hard man who was reputed to be vicious in a gun fight. He was fast and he was deadly. He quite often shot a wounded adversary right between the eyes as a lasting memento to all would see the body. These men were out and out dangerous.

The one thought present in Doc Simmons' mind as he climbed aboard the horse that the two men had commandeered for him was that,

"I hope that Cole Stockton can read the signs that I left for him."

* *

Hanna James slowly waddled her way up the stairs to Doctor Simmons' office with her husband's assistance. She was due to deliver their first baby in a week and she wanted to have the Doc take one last look at her for re-assurance.

The young couple reached the door to the Doctor's office and, to their surprise, found it slightly ajar. They entered to find an empty office. Doctor Simmons was nowhere to be found.

Hanna sat down with a forlorn look on her face. Charlie James spoke comforting words to her and gently held her hand. "Don't worry Hanna. The Doc has probably just gone to the store for something. He'll probably be back within a few minutes."

However, the young couple waited for over an hour and still no sign of Doctor Simmons.

"Charlie, I want you to go and look for him. It ain't like Doc Simmons to not be here——especially when he knew that I was coming to see him this morning."

Charlie James nodded his agreement. He gently squeezed Hanna's hand and softly told her that he would look for the doctor. He went out the door, down the steps, and started to walk the entire town.

He walked up the boardwalk to the end of town looking into shop windows. He walked down the other side looking into shop windows, the general mercantile, saloons, and finally, the livery stable. Everyone he encountered had the same answer, they had not seen Doc Simmons today.

Charlie James took one look through the stalls, then, hurried to the jail in search of Sheriff J.C. Kincaid.

* *

J.C. Kincaid and I were enjoying a peaceful game of chess and drinking his latest idea of good coffee when the door opened and Charlie James stepped into the Miller's Station jail.

He had a puzzled look on his face.

"Something I can help you with, Charlie?" asked J.C.

"Good Morning Sheriff Kincaid——Marshal Stockton. Yes. Hanna had an appointment with Doc Simmons this morning. We got there on time, but old Doc Simmons wasn't there. We waited for over an hour and he still didn't show up. Hanna sent me to looking for him and I went up one side of the street and down the other. He is nowhere in this town. Something is mighty peculiar about all this. I stopped at the livery and Doc Simmons' horse is still in her stall. I remember, also, that when I left his office that his buggy is still parked in the alley like it usually is. I fear that something must have happened to him."

I looked at J.C. and he looked at me. "Let's take a walk J.C.," I said, "That certainly is not like Doc Simmons and I've a sudden thought. Do you remember that wire from three days ago?"

"Yah, Cole. Do you think that them boys could have made it all the way down here with a couple of wounded men and avoided that posse that was after them?"

"Stranger things have happened. But, I seem to recall that some of them boys know the wild trails where one can travel virtually unseen and untracked by a posse unfamiliar with the terrain. I want to see that office."

J.C. Kincaid and I strode out of the jail and down to Doc Simmons' office with worried Charlie James almost running to keep up with us.

We entered the office to find Hanna sitting there with a most disappointed look on her young face.

"Good morning, Hanna. You look simply radiant today. When did you say that little rascal was going to be born?"

A big smile lit across her freckled face. "Good morning, Marshal Stockton——Sheriff Kincaid. Thank you for asking again. I'm due to deliver our first child next Friday. I am sure that it will be a boy. I'm carrying him low and he sure kicks out now and then."

I looked at her and grinned, "I know you're looking for Doc Simmons and he isn't here right now. But, we'll find him for you."

On a second thought, I asked, "Hanna", I asked, "Have you had breakfast yet?"

"Why, no, Marshal Stockton, I haven't eaten much of anything this morning yet."

"Why, Hanna! A young woman like you, carrying a child has just got to eat something every morning. After all, you are eating for TWO now. Tell you what, why don't Charlie just take you on down to the restaurant and order you some bacon, eggs, hotcakes with maple syrup, fresh biscuits, a glass of fresh milk, and whatever fresh berries that they have on special this morning. Tell them to put it on the Sheriff's tab."

Hanna perked up considerably and looked deeply in Charlie's worried eyes. She got up and waddled out the door with him.

J.C. Kincaid looked at me and said, "I sure like the way that you just spend my hard earned budget money, Cole. Doggone it, you know that I'm trying to save every penny so's Louise and I can get married."

"Aw, J.C., don't worry. I'll have the Marshal's Denver office pay you for the bill."

"Cole. Dammit. The last time you did something like this, it was over three months before I got my money back."

"Well, J.C., look at it this way. It's going to a very good cause, and we need privacy to look over this here office. I want time to look over everything."

J.C. sighed and nodded his agreement. We spent the next hour just looking at things in the office. We dared not touch anything.

Within an hour, we noticed that some things were missing that should be well stocked in a frontier Doctor's Office, that being namely laudanum, a form of opium that was used as anesthetic when operating. There was none.

The next things missing were rolled bandages and thick pads for blotting wounds. There were none of these either.

The doctor's black bag had disappeared, as well as several other instruments that I recall that he used for operations such as removing lead bullets from gunshot wounds.

I turned to J.C. and gave him my surmise.

"J.C., I think that Doctor Simmons has been taken by someone——and I think that those that took him are the same bunch that the posse from Fort Collins was looking for. That posse lost them boys after a hot fifty mile chase. They thought that at least three or four of the outlaws were hit, and now I feel certain that they took Doc Simmons to care for them. I plan to ride into the wilds within the hour to see if I can run across a trail or two. Get a message to Laura for me, will you? Tell her that I won't be there for supper tonight, and maybe even for a few more nights. While you are at it, wire Toby Bodine up in Creede and tell him to ride on down here straight away. I may need him."

J.C. Kincaid nodded his head to the affirmative, adding, "I'll also tell Hanna and Charlie that Doc Simmons had to go on an urgent medical call in the wilds where horse and buggy couldn't go."

"Good thought, J.C. Thanks."

I strode on down to the general mercantile and ordered my supplies for five days in the wilds. The young female clerk sort of looked at me with soulful eyes.

"I hope that you catch whoever you are after, Marshal."

"So do I, Katherine. So do I."

CHAPTER FOURTEEN

Wounded Outlaws

Doc Simmons and the two outlaws rode hard into the early morning and by noon they were deep into the wilds of the Lower Colorado Territory. Doc tried to remember approximately where they were at all times. He tried to recognize landmarks. Doc Simmons also knew that if he should try to escape that these men would hunt him down and kill him. He had to have some idea of where he was at and how far they had traveled in order to seek shelter and take evasive action should the occasion arise.

He wondered also if U.S. Marshal Cole Stockton would be able to read the subtle signs in his office and know where the outlaws were headed.

Just after two in the afternoon, Harley Judson called a slow walk with the horses and they entered into the thickest brush, pine stands, and aspen groves that Doc Simmons had ever witnessed.

They made their way through the thick underbrush, and finally, Doc Simmons caught the scent of burning wood. A campfire lay dead ahead.

Fifteen minutes later the thick undergrowth and forest gave way to a small clearing and Doc saw first hand what he was up against.

Twelve men sat around in this ragtag camp and five of them displayhed pain because of various wounds evidenced by the dirty, bloody rags wrapped around them.

"My God," thought Carlin Simmons as he viewed the wounded men.

These were rough men. They were filthy men, having not changed their clothing in weeks. They reeked of liquor, tobacco, powder smoke, and of the pure hard stench of sweat.

Harley halted them and stepped down from his horse. He motioned Doc Simmons to do likewise. He pointed to the wounded men who lay in various places all around the camp.

Harley turned to those men that were unharmed and commanded, "This here is a doctor. When it comes to tending those in need, he will be the authority. Elsewise, I am the boss. Whatever this here medicine man needs, within reason, you will get it and you will help him. Our wounded kin will live because we do what this man asks. Any of you cross me and Doc will be digging lead out of you, too. What is it that you need firstly, Doc?"

Doctor Carlin Simmons swallowed hard. This was a scene from the past. Visions of the carnage of the War between the states rose before his eyes.

So, he closed his eyes for a long moment and suddenly could easily visualize Gettysburg where wounded men lay scattered all over the field of battle. A shudder ran through him.

"You need to gather up all of these wounded men and put them all in one small area where I can easily move from one to the other." He looked over the area and then, motioned with his right hand. "Yes——— over there, under those aspen. Secondly, I will need a good hot fire and several pans of boiling water. I want their clothes taken off and I want them under blankets. These men have got to be cleaned up before I can operate and take the lead out've them. Thirdly, I will need all the clean bandages you have got, or I will need all of the clean shirts that you others can spare, and I do mean clean—freshly washed."

"You are mighty wishful, Doc," said Harley. "This here ain't no regular hospital. You will have to make do. We ain't undressing them, and we ain't washing them."

Doc Simmons felt himself grow impatient, "Then at least, take off their damn boots, spurs and socks. You make sure that I have plenty of hot water. I will clean them up where I have to work."

"Don't get feisty with me, Doc. I'd not rather do it, but Ole Cooley there is just itching to cause pain on someone, and for some reason——he hates Doctors. Just be mighty careful how you talk to me."

"Harley, I'll talk to you anyway that I want. I am the doctor here, and if you want any of these men to live, you will do as I say."

Harley suddenly whipped out his Colt and angrily tapped Doc Simmons along the side of his head. Simmons fell to his knees and cried out with pain. He held the side of his head. A trickle of blood ran from the sudden split on his temple.

"Now then, <u>Doctor</u>. I will say it only once again. This ain't no hospital. Cut them there bullets out, patch them up and we will be gone. We will leave you here——alive. You don't do it, I'll leave your dead carcass for the scavengers."

Suddenly one of the wounded men cried out in gut-retching pain.

"God, Harley. Get that doctor over here. I am bleeding to death inside. Harley, for God's sake, help me."

Harley looked over at the young man and his face turned soft——eyes almost misty. "Hang on there, Scott. The doctor is here. He will be with you in only a few minutes. He'll fix you up."

Simmons looked straight into Harley Judson's eyes and knew. This wounded man was Judson's youngest brother. He nodded and rose to his feet. He pushed on past Harley and kneeled beside the wounded man.

He lifted the blanket from the stricken man and almost choked. The man had been shot in the stomach with a rifle at fairly close range.

Infection and gangrene had already set in, and there was nothing that could be done. The man had only a matter of a day, if that, of dying.

The young man couldn't have been more than seventeen. He looked up into Doc Simmons' eyes with a long pleading look. Doctor Simmons knew the pain that the man was going through.

"I need my bag," Doc called out over his shoulder.

"Get it, Cooley," Harley Judson commanded.

Cooley Blaine reluctantly retrieved the black bag from the doctor's horse and walking up to him thrust it hard at the doctor. He had an evil like grin on his face.

Cooley whispered softly to Doc Simmons, "He's a goner, ain't he, Doc? I can almost smell the death. I was at Gettysburg, and I ain't smelled that smell again until just yesterday. This man is infected with the gangrene and will die. When he dies, you die."

"Cooley knows," thought Doctor Carlin Simmons. "He knows that most of these men are going to die and he is just biding time. He wants to blame their deaths on me, and then justify killing me. I wonder just how long I can hold out."

Doc Simmons' thoughts briefly turned to his one salvation, Cole——Cole Stockton! Where are you? I am somewhere in the wilds and you have got to find us before it is too late."

* *

U.S. Marshal Cole Stockton sat his dark chestnut Warrior at the edge of the wilds and pondered the situation.

"If I were to kidnap a doctor and a lot of medical supplies, where would I take him to? That's easy. I would take him to a group of wounded outlaws. Where could I hold a group of, say, eight men and keep their whereabouts from prying eyes. It would have to be the roughest country that a man could travel. They would be in country that no one would really want to go into. They would be headed toward the passes south, but couldn't have entered yet. No. They are more toward north, close to the forests and possibly on high ground with a lot of cover. They would be at a place with the thickest of growth and where they could observe any riders for miles. I'd bet that those men are close to only twenty-five miles from me right now. I guess the best way is to work south to north and watch for tracks of fast moving horses."

Cole clucked to Warrior and worked his way north. He rode slowly, taking in every movement, every stillness, everything that looked out of place. Now and then he would dismount and examine the ground closely. He shook his head.

By dusk, he had not found that which he sought. He decided to turn upward along the slopes of the steep foothills of the Rockies and to watch the distance for even the slightest flicker of a campfire.

Darkness enveloped the land and movement became dangerous. Stockton cautiously picked his way through the thick underbrush and closely spaced stands of pine and aspen. He worked his way up the slope until he dared not go any further. Even one as experienced as himself would be foolishly daring death to find him should he continue.

He took a deep breath, sighed, and dismounted. He stripped his saddle and gear off Warrior and let him graze delightfully at the tall lush grasses of the mountain slope.

Cole placed his gear against a thick aspen and wearily sat down. He had covered a lot of territory this day and still he hadn't found even the slightest clue of hoof prints. He closed his eyes for a long moment and silently thought of the woman who stirred his blood with only a moment's look from her crystal blue eyes.

He smiled for a long minute, then grimaced. He swallowed hard. He could almost taste the stew that Laura Sumner was sure to have on the stove. He thought of the fresh biscuits that were sure to accompany the stew. He thought of the berry pie that might be waiting afterward.

He was suddenly hungry. He reached into his saddlebags and withdrew a large piece of dried beef jerky and ripped off a large bite. He reached to his canteen and took a long swallow. The juices of the jerky and water combined tasted sort of like a beef broth and that brought more thoughts of a fine stew with fresh vegetables and large cuts of tender beef.

Cole Stockton sighed. Any normal man would be sitting across a finely prepared table, looking a good woman in the face and devouring his fill of a spicy, flavorful stew.

Instead, here he sat with his back against a cold tree trunk, chewing on tough dried beef jerky and drinking warm water from a canteen.

"Just why the Hell do I do this?" he thought to himself. He glanced down at his vest and at the Silver Star pinned to it.

"You do it because you are the best man for the job. Folks depend on you for justice. All right, Cole Stockton! That's enough of that wallowing in self thought. Only one man is going to find them scavengers and the Doc, and that is you. Get busy and think. Where are they?"

He rose suddenly and walked quietly all around his position. The moon was not yet up and it was like the black hole of Hell in the wilds.

Cole Stockton listened intently. He could hear the slight scurry of night creatures, he heard the sudden call of the horned owl as its yellowish eyes searched the night for a tasty meal. The absence of these sounds would signal imminent danger.

It was just a slight flicker, then it was gone.

Stockton pondered it hard.

That flicker appeared to be about twenty miles to the north and on the same slope line that he now stood. It was a chance.

He watched the direction intently for the next five long minutes. Nothing!

"Perhaps," he thought, "it is only wishful thinking."

Just as Stockton turned away, a flash of brightness grew from the darkness.

It grew brighter for a long moment, then was just as suddenly swallowed up by a cloak of darkness. He continued to watch.

Minutes later a slight eerie glow shined in the distance. He shook his head.

"That's them. Someone just threw another log on the fire and someone else rolled it away. That glow is from the coals of a smoldering fire just hot enough to heat water, sterilize instruments, and to keep a slight warmth in the air. That's got to be them."

Cole momentarily felt the chill in the air. In October, the nights and early mornings were quite cold in the mountain areas of Colorado.

He went to his gear, took out his bedroll and wrapped himself up for the night. He knew about where that campfire was and he was going to be there by mid-afternoon or early evening.

He placed his Winchester close to hand and as a second measure, slid his Colt out of the holster and placed it within easy reach under the blanket. He had learned long ago that one could not be too careful for this place was the wilds and anything was possible.

* *

Carlin Simmons moved slowly from one wounded man to the other.

Of the five wounded men only two would survive for more than one day.

Doctor Simmons did the best that he could to make the doomed men comfortable and supplied them with enough laudanum to dull the pain that they were enduring.

He silently grew angry at these men. Had they left the wounded men to the clemency of the posse they might have lived. He shook his head. This scene was a senseless waste of human life, all because of a close-knit family attempting to save their kin from prosecution.

Doc thought hard, "Three of these wounded men are going to die shortly. I must make like they are still alive and treat them as if they are under the power of the drug. As long as the others think them still alive, I have a chance to live myself. I just don't know what else to do. I pray that Cole Stockton has read the signs and is on his way here. These men are vicious and it is evident that they have no regard for human life, except for their own. I have got to have faith to bear this terrible burden."

Carlin Simmons said a silent prayer and suddenly a flutter ran through his body. It might have seemed to the others that he was quivering with the cold, but he knew better. It was at that very moment that he knew.

He knew that Cole Stockton was only a matter of a few miles from him and was coming to his aid.

Doc Simmons thought again. "When Stockton gets here, this campsite is going to become a battle-ground. I have got to think of a plan. I must flatten myself to the ground and find some type of shelter. Stockton is going to come straight on in here, that's his way, and he is going to shoot every mother's son that is standing. When he is outnumbered, he wastes no bullets. He will shoot every living thing that moves until it don't move no more."

His thoughts continued, "The other thing is Harley. If he finds that his youngest brother is dead, he will kill me. Cooley Blaine wants to kill me straight out. If he gets the chance, he will. I hate it, but I must find myself a gun. I may have to use it to protect myself and these other wounded men that might live. I must be brave. Lord, give me the strength to do what must be done."

* *

I had a fairly good idea from the flicker that I had seen last night as to the whereabouts of that outlaw gang and Doc.

I mounted Warrior and we took a brisk stride toward that site.

Word had it that several of the gang were wounded and I feared for Doc Simmons. I'd also heard that these men were most vicious when it came to fighting for their miserable lives. This gang was made up mostly of kinfolk from the Tennessee and Arkansas area, and them kinfolk carried many a grudge———often to the point of death. They would be a stubborn lot and the thought that I might just have to kill all of them entered my mind.

Well, I'd faced such odds before, but never with the life of a hostage such as a doctor hanging in the balance. My method would have to be swift and sure.

Of one thing, I could be assured. Once the ball opened, there would be no time to seek out the good souls from the bad. My plan was simple. I would ride right in there and shoot everything that moved. A lonely shudder ran through my body at that point and I wondered,

"Cole Stockton, are you good enough? Can you save Doc, or will you just get him killed? I would think on that point all the way up to that camp."

Chapter Fifteen

Toby Bodine

The shadow of a lone rider passed silently through the tree lines of the Lower Colorado forests of pine and aspen. He watched the signs carefully as he rode. He had been scarcely six hours in the saddle when he crossed the tracks of a band of horsemen. The signs looked suspicious.

They were moving slowly and every so often, he found splotches of dried blood on the ground.

The group of riders that he followed tended to an awful lot of wounded men.

The lanky young rider named Toby Bodine thought repeatedly about the bank robbers he'd heard so much about as he followed the closely spaced prints.

Suddenly, he pulled up short on his reins. An uneasy feeling surged through his body. He drew his Winchester, then eased forward in a state of readiness.

* *

Miles away, Doctor Carlin Simmons compassionately cared for the wounded men while at the same time his eyes secretly and carefully searched the campsite.

He knew that he needed a safe place to slide into when the anticipated ruckus started. Doc Simmons also noticed that none of the wounded were armed, or so he thought.

When he started to move Scott Judson to a more comfortable position, he felt something hard under the young outlaw's body. Scott lay on a Colt revolver that seemed to have been overlooked by those that disarmed the wounded.

Carlin Simmons closed his eyes for a long moment. "Dare I even touch this gun? Is it loaded? If I take it now, where will I hide it?"

He had no reason to kill. He only wanted to protect himself and to stall those that he knew might want to kill him.

He needed to buy time for Cole Stockton to get to him.

Another thought struck him, "No. I can't. I don't want Stockton to get to me. That's where all the returning fire will be aimed at. I've got to stay away from Stockton until the fight is over. I need to be absolutely still until that time. I can't draw attention to myself."

Simmons slowly looked up to the ridge above them. He thought he saw an ever so slight movement. He thought, "Maybe just a deer, or wolf, or—or——something."

He closed his eyes for a moment, then opened them again. He scanned the area carefully. There was not the slightest movement.

"I must be seeing things. A man gets that way when he is exhausted. I must take a few minutes to nap."

Doc Simmons moved to his blankets and lay down. He closed his eyes and softly drifted into the world of dreams.

* *

Warrior and I rode steadily toward the flickering that I detected last night. The going was hard and slow. Whoever led this bunch knew exactly what the terrain was like, and it would be almost impossible for a full posse to approach them without being seen or heard.

Evening came once again, and what seemed to be a little more than twenty five miles at first, turned into more like fifty miles, up slope and picking easy through nature's hell.

I looked around me then and I knew this land. The thought hit me.

"Cole Stockton, you are a crazy man. No man in his right mind would travel the wilds at night."

Nonetheless, I ventured onward through dusk into dark, stopping Warrior only long enough to rest him and partake of a few bites of my tough trail jerky. The fate of a good doctor held in the balance, and I thought about what Doc might be thinking.

"He knows me. He will know that I will come directly into them and offer the challenge. I will give them the chance to throw down their arms or take lead. Doctor Simmons has dug more than enough lead out've my prisoners to know this. Yes. With luck, I will be at that campsite before dawn, and then, all hell is going to break loose." Confidence in his plan encouraged Cole.

* *

Toby Bodine wearily dismounted from his bay horse and moved warily forward to the edge of the cliffs. He stopped for a long moment while the smell of wood smoke filtered into his nostrils.

"Whoever they are, they've camped. Reason tells me that these are the men from that bank holdup, and they are tending to their wounded. If this is the case, there are too many for me to take on alone. I will lie low and watch them. Sometime, a posse will catch up to us and we will take them. I wonder! Is this is the reason that Cole wired me to come to the passes? That would be like him. He wants me to get between them and the pass into New Mexico. But what if, this is that gang? If it is, then Cole Stockton is going to ride right into that mess once he finds them, and then let the Good Lord sort out the bodies and souls later. No. I'll just stay here and watch them."

Deputy U.S. Marshal Toby Bodine lay back against a tall pine and casually watched the activity. From his advantage point, he figured that he was a mere four hundred feet sloped above the gang, and he could see——everything.

With the last rays of dusk, a slight movement caught Toby Bodine's eyes. He glinted a bit, then shielded his eyes from the receding sun. A last second glint on something shiny held his eyes for a moment.

Then, he made it out. It was a single man on horseback and he was slowly working his way toward the campsite.

He was working his way so as to not come up suddenly on the camp, but to circumvent it and come in from a blind side.

Toby Bodine grinned widely. He knew the pattern. He saw also that this rider would come across the gang's picketed horses before he would reach the camp. That rider could be none other than Cole Stockton.

Toby knew the drill very well. As the early morning rays lit the mountain side, the camp below would awaken to the sound of a soft voice. He could almost imagine it in his mind.

"U.S. Marshal. Drop your guns, grab sky, or take lead." The gang would be tired and worn, with sleep reddened eyes. Some would be dazed, confused, and throw down their guns immediately.

Then, then——there were the others. There were those that no matter the consequence would drag iron, and that's when Toby meant to be right down there at the edge of that campsite.

He decided to take a short nap. This was too good to be true. The entire holdup gang in one swoop. He closed his eyes.

A gravelly voice suddenly sneered, "Well, now! What have we here? A young whelp with a star on his chest. Looks like he fancy's hisself to be a lawman. What say we disarm this young man, take his star and drag his carcass down to the camp?"

* *

Toby Bodine's eyes shot open at the words, and looked directly into the ugliest mean faces that he had ever seen.

Luke Danson and Chuck Gaines had also seen the slight movement above their camp and advised Harley.

Harley told them to "sly" themselves out of camp and come up on that spot from a blind side to check it out.

"All right, whelp! Get up and hand over that hardware. You were so curious about our camp, we'll take you down there."

Toby Bodine thought quickly and grinned widely.

"Well, Howdy boys! You are absolutely correct. I do want to go down there and check out your campsite; however, seeing that I am a

Deputy United States Marshal, both of you two are under arrest. Drop your guns and I won't have to shoot you."

Chuck Gaines laughed heartily, "Boy, you shore got some nerve. We got the drop on you. Our guns are out and pointed. You make one move, we going to shoot the living daylights out've you."

"I figured as much, but first, you got to cock them single shot revolvers."

The two Arkansas outlaws glanced at each other, then peeked at their revolvers.

In that one split second, that was all it took.

In the next instant, Bodine's hands flashed to his own holster, and he rolled hard to left. Fire and hot lead spit from the bore of his Colt.

The two outlaws slammed backward with each round as Toby Bodine fanned his Colt at close range.

Toby slowly got to his feet. Both men were stone cold dead. Toby hung his head and whispered softly to himself, "Just like Cole taught me! There is always one split second in which you have the advantage, DON'T WASTE IT. Damn it, I just spoiled Cole's surprise visit, they will be expecting someone now. No! Maybe, just maybe, if I go down there, they will think that I am alone. I'm going on down there and challenge them."

Toby Bodine made his way down the treacherous path and, once below, found himself within fifty yards of the camp. He moved forward with Colt drawn. When near enough and able to recognize figures around the camp, he stood up and announced his challenge,

"United States Marshal, drop yore guns or take lead!"

Immediately, something or someone rushed up behind him and a brilliant light flashed before his eyes. Toby Bodine slipped to the ground, unconscious.

* *

Doc Simmons looked up to see two men carrying a trussed up limp body. They carried him to the wounded section in the camp and just dumped him on the ground in front of Carlin Simmons.

Harley spoke, "Bring him around and fix up that cut on his head, Doc. I got to ask him a couple of questions." Doc Simmons reached into his black bag and produced a small bottle of smelling salts. He held it close the young deputy's nostrils.

Toby Bodine suddenly made a face and struggled against the bonds that held him securely. Suddenly, the throbbing pain shot through his head. "God, what hit me?"

"I did," grinned Cooley Blaine. "I wanted to just shoot you, but the boss over there wanted you alive. How did you happen to take down them two up there on the ridge? Both of them was quite known for being good with firearms?"

Bodine looked defiantly up into Cooley's cold eyes. "They may have been good, but they were stupid. I guess they must be kin to you."

Cooley took a quick step forward and kicked the young deputy in the groin. He then drew his Colt and cocked the hammer back.

"I'll show you stupid! Get ready to meet yore maker, smart mouth."

"COOLEY! Holster that hogleg! I'll take it from here. All right, young deputy. Just who are you and where are you from? How many are with you and where are they? How did you find us? Don't give me no sass or I'll let Cooley finish what he wanted to do," Harley fired the only questions this time.

"Go to hell!" Toby spoke defiantly.

Harley reached down and grabbed the tied up Toby Bodine by the shirtfront, then plowed a fist into his mouth. Toby grunted with the impact, recoiled, then spit blood from his mouth.

Doctor Simmons winced, then just blurted it out, "He's Deputy U.S. Marshal Toby Bodine. He normally stays up around Creede. Probably on his way down to our town Miller's Station near the passes and came across your trail. This many wounded men has got to leave a blood trail somewhere."

Harley reflected on that.

"That right, sassy young Marshal? You find blood on the trail and follow the signs?"

"It wasn't hard, even for one as inexperienced as me. After the first five miles, I figured out who you were. I tracked you here. There is no one else——backtrack my horse if you don't believe me, but there are a dozen posses out looking for you. One of them is sure to run across that trail also. I just happened to get lucky."

"Lucky? I would say that it was your most unlucky day to find that trail. All right, Doc, fix him up, but he stays tied. I may want to talk to him some more before this is over."

Harley and the rest moved back to the center of the camp and poured themselves cups of coffee.

Doctor Simmons looked down at Toby Bodine and just shook his head.

"Toby, just what has gotten into you? You know that you couldn't take on this entire camp by yourself. Not to say that you ain't good, but these here men are uncaring about who or what they kill. Here, this is going to sting."

Doc Simmons placed a swab of liniment against Toby's busted lip and grinned a bit as Toby winced loudly, and his eyes watered.

"Serves you right for not getting help instead of shooting down them boys up there and then coming right on down here like a fool."

Toby looked straight into Doc Simmons' eyes and smiled slightly.

Then Carlin Simmons saw the sparkle in Toby's eyes. This kid had deliberately come into this camp to distract them. Something was up. A quick tremor shot straight up the Doctor's spine.

He suddenly remembered that Toby had been high on the ridge. He could see things up there that no one down here could possibly know.

Carlin Simmons looked straight into Toby's eyes and silently formed the name on his lips——Cole Stockton?

Toby never moved his head, but Carlin Simmons could read his eyes. Toby winked at him. Doc Simmons whispered to him as he tended the deep cut on the young Marshal's head. "Toby, there is a hand gun underneath young Scott over there. Don't worry, he's dead, died about two hours ago, but they don't know. When Cole rides in here, we have got to get down and stay down. You know how Cole is. He is going to shoot everything that moves."

"No, Doc. We are going to shoot everything that moves. You keep that scalpel handy. When the time is right, you slice these ropes and dive for cover, cause I'm going after that gun. There will be a hot time in the ole camp right about daybreak."

CHAPTER SIXTEEN

Justice Comes at Dawn

I moved steady and carefully toward the general area of last night's flicker when a slight, but familiar sound caught my ears.

I drew Warrior up short and he stood as still as a mouse watching a cat pad on by. The sound echoed and then I knew.

That was gunfire! About five miles further through the roughest of the wilds and up high.

I thought considerable about that. I wondered just who or what would fire that many rounds in succession. It sounded almost like someone was "fanning" a Colt. Then, nothing but silence.

Darkness was falling once again, but this time, I stayed in the saddle and slowly picked my way toward the spot I had in mind.

Suddenly, Warrior stopped dead in his tracks. I caught the scent at the same time. It smelled like wood smoke, and not too far ahead.

I dismounted and softly spoke to Warrior, "Stay here, Boy. I'll call you when I want you."

The big chestnut bobbed his head up and down as if he understood, then turned to munch on some tall fescue.

Smiling, I shook my head, then walked to his side and withdrew my Winchester. I also got my spare Colt revolver from the saddle bags.

That horse! He got to eat whilst I had to go without and move forward toward the high possibility of immediate danger.

I thought then that I might like to come back in a second life as a horse. The thought made me chuckle silently to myself.

I stealthily made my way forward and momentarily, I caught the strong odor of horses. I stood extremely still, then sticking my index finger into my mouth to wet it, I raised it into the air. Luck was with me——I was downwind from them. I continued forward until I found them. I went to the cool ground and lay there for a while unmoving. I wanted to see if there were any guards on these horses.

I waited for half an hour and saw no one.

These arrogant guys were mighty sure of themselves. I stood slightly and moved to within the horse herd. There were fifteen animals in all. I spoke softly and soothingly to the animals as I moved between them to the darkened edges of the camp.

I could make out a group of men lying on the ground straight across from me. I saw Doc Simmons tending to someone. Those must the wounded men.

I got another good look and recognized Toby Bodine! He was trussed up like a pig to market.

It must have been Toby that had "fanned" that Colt, like some kind of signal, then got himself captured.

I scanned the entire camp, visualizing every bit of cover that one of these men could move to. There were five able-bodied outlaw killers huddled around that fire drinking coffee and eating. They were up and alert right now.

I decided to move closer with the early gray of dawn.

I thought also of how I might get a revolver into Toby's hands. I sure could use the help.

* *

In the still gray of early morning, cold dew, almost a slight frost, covered the ground of the Lower Colorado wilds. The outlaw camp lay quiet. Two men sat near the fire holding their hands to the warmth of the smoldering coals. One looked at the other, "Sam, it's light enough now, so let's put a log on them coals and get some real warmth around us."

Sam Madden nodded his approval to his partner, Jerrod Whitlow, with a shiver. He shrugged out of his heavy coat and reached for a good-sized log.

At that very moment a tall dark shadow stepped out of the surrounding darkness of the tree line. He held a Winchester rifle in his hands and his eyes had the distinct look of unbridled determination.

The shadow suddenly chambered a live round into the Winchester's firing mechanism. The sound of metal sliding against metal eerily sliced the crisp morning air, followed by, "U.S. Marshal! Drop your guns and grab sky. Them that don't will meet your Maker!"

Jerrod Whitlow jumped up and as he did so his right hand moved to his Colt. Sam Madden also turned and his icy cold fingers slipped to his holster.

Two sharp cracks broke the silence and then the entire camp became a beehive of men scrambling for cover, fumbling for weapons, and screaming out in pain as the unmistakable thud of rifle lead tore into their bodies.

Whitlow was the first to feel the hot burn of heavy lead tear into his chest. His revolver was almost out of the holster when the bullet slammed him hard and literally threw him backward into the smoldering coals of the fire.

Sam Madden took the next one through his left side. He grunted with the hot burn and lurched to the right. Another round smacked into his chest and he spit blood as he fell violently to the ground. He lay there screaming for Doc to come and save him.

* *

Doctor Carlin Simmons lay half awake, trembling in the cold wet morning when the soft voice issued the challenge. His eyes shot wide open and he looked all around the camp. He suddenly saw Cole Stockton emerge from the shadows and just as suddenly Cole's Winchester spit orange flame and hot lead.

Doc Simmons rolled over to come face to face with a widely grinning Toby Bodine. "Hurry, Doc, slice these ropes with that scalpel. I got to get that revolver."

Carlin Simmons fumbled slightly, but managed to hold on to the scalpel that he had slid into his coat pocket. In one quick slice, the ropes fell away from Toby's wrists and he wasted no time.

He immediately rolled away from Doc Simmons, stooped slightly, then dived over the body of Scott Judson. Toby rolled Scott's body quickly away and grasped the revolver. He flipped open the loading gate and checked the loads. It was live and ready.

Toby stretched out behind Scott's body and began to look for targets of his own. His eyes searched for one figure in particular——— Cooley Blaine. He found him.

Cooley had dived behind a fallen tree and was frantically looking for a way to the horses, but Cole Stockton stood between the camp and the picketed horses.

Suddenly, Cooley looked straight in the direction of Doc Simmons.

A broad crooked grin spread across his face. Cooley began working his way toward the area of the fallen, wounded men while Toby Bodine intently followed Cooley's every move.

Cooley was within thirty yards of Doc Simmons when he suddenly stood up and yelled at the medicine man, "Told you I hated Doctors. I'm going to blow your brains out, Doc."

Cooley cocked the hammer back on his Colt and lined straight up on Simmons middle. Just as he pulled the trigger, a hard, searing fire drove through his own gut and Cooley Blaine jerked back with the impact. His finger tightened on the trigger of his Colt and he fired wild, the bullet smacking into the nearest pine.

Cooley's eyes went wide as he felt the second hammer of death slam into his chest. He jerked once again, then went to his knees. He struggled to get up. He dropped his head and took a couple of deep breaths. He looked up then to see Toby Bodine standing twenty yards in front of him. A third bullet hit Cooley and he died before he hit the ground.

Harley Judson and Wes Madsen were facing a fullisade of hot lead flying in their direction just as fast as Cole Stockton could fire that Winchester. When the empty "click" sounded, Stockton immediately dropped the Winchester to the ground, and a split second later, both of his hands were filled with Colt revolvers, spitting fire and hot lead.

Wes Madsen screamed as one round took him in the middle. A moment later, another round drove dead center into his chest and he stumbled backward, staggering. A third round closely followed the second and jerked him to his toes for a second. He doubled over and fell face down in the dirt.

Harley Judson was fighting mad. He grimaced, screamed a death threat, then stood up to meet his adversary face to face. He never knew what hit him.

Stockton's bullet spun directly into his body. Harley's finger tightened around the trigger of his revolver and it discharged into the ground as a second bullet bolted into his chest.

That bullet was followed by a third and a fourth, until Harley Judson collided with the ground shot to doll rags.

When a deathly silence fell over the camp, Cole Stockton's eyes swept the area. He holstered his right hand Colt and flipped open the loading gate of his spare. He calmly punched out six empty shells and reloaded six fresh ones. He shoved the warm Colt into his belt and drawing his primary weapon, repeated the action. He stepped forward to examine each and every one of the hapless outlaws.

Toby Bodine slowly approached Cooley Blaine and looked down on his broken and lifeless body. "The score is settled, Cooley. Burn in Hell."

Doc Simmons slowly stood up and looked around. He shook his head. He had never before witnessed a gunfight such as this. He had several times had to take lead out of one or more of Cole Stockton's prisoners and now he finally understood the man. Cole Stockton outnumbered five to one, had just walked right in and shot hell out of every man that stood and drew arms against him.

Of the five worthy outlaws in the beginning, only one still lived.

Sam Madden miraculously still lay on the cold morning ground laboring for life. His eyes were filled with pain and he whispered for the doctor. Doc Simmons moved to the man's side, tore open his shirt, and examined both wounds. He closed his eyes for a moment, then looked Sam directly in the eyes.

"I can't help you, Sam. You are bleeding to death inside. You may have only an hour to live."

"What about my brother, Doc? The one with the red shirt. You fixed him up, didn't you?"

"Sam, your brother died during the fight. You will join him shortly. I'm sorry, but I don't know of any way that can save you."

"Thanks, Doc. You are honest. At least, I will join my brother and we will walk the streets of Hell together. Don't fret none, Doc. I had a feeling when we took on this bank job that neither of us would come back. I understand, Doc, that I have been shot down by one of the best marshals in the Territory, is that true?"

"Yes, Sam. You were shot down by U.S. Marshal Cole Stockton."

"Cole Stockton! I've heard the stories. He is as good as they say, ain't he?"

"Sometimes too good, Sam. I've taken lead out of many that resisted him. Too bad that you didn't just throw down your gun. You'd still be alive."

"Doc, don't blame him. We——I——well, we just thought ourselves bullet proof. You know how it is. Promise me that I will be buried with my brother, please."

"All right, Sam. My promise."

Sam took one last deep breath and closed his eyes. His soul slipped silently out of his body and joined that of his brother.

Two spirits then looked toward a lonely man who stood near the campfire with his head bowed slightly and they read his mind. They felt the Hell fire of his soul and knew the pain that flowed through his veins.

Shortly thereafter, a warm presence filled his soul——the thought of a woman and her vision slowly drifted into sight.

The vision of two souls embraced and a warmth flowed between them, an eternal warmth. Their own souls began fading into a world unknown to them.

Cole Stockton stood near the fire warming his hands. His eyes were closed and he was thinking deeply about Laura Sumner. The warmth came and flooded his soul.

* *

Cole Stockton, Toby Bodine, and Doc Simmons stood looking around the outlaw camp. Of the five wounded outlaws, none had survived. Of the seven able-bodied outlaws, none survived.

Doc Simmons looked up into Cole Stockton's eyes. He saw the anguish that lay behind his mind.

"Cole, I have to confess. I've dug lead out've you and I've dug lead out've some of those you brought in. My life has been dedicated to life and I didn't understand why most of them had to be shot. Now, I do. These men were killers. They never cared who they hurt, they never cared about their own kin enough to leave them for medical treatment——even at the cost of prison. I can't say that any man deserves to die, but you did right. These men would have killed all three of us and never batted an eyelash."

Doctor Carlin Simmons closed his eyes for a long moment before continuing, "My God! I was at Gettysburg, but I have never in my life seen a gunfight such as this. These men were shot and still, for the most part, with their dying breath wanted to take you both with them. I now understand. Forgive me, Cole. Forgive me, Toby. It takes a certain kind of man to face this element day in and day out. I saw the look in your eyes, Cole, as you were shooting them. I saw the pain, but yet I saw the justice in it. I saw the hell fires of your soul. I also know those fires."

The three men stood silent for a long minute.

It was Cole who spoke first. "Doc, we got to get back towards town. Hanna James is due to deliver anytime now and I just know that Charlie will go nuts without you there."

"The hell with town, Cole. Let's ride straight to their homestead. I got everything with me that I will need."

"Toby, I hate to leave you with this mess, but can you do it? Pack all these bodies up on their horses and bring them into town."

"Don't worry about me none, Cole. I'll be about three or four hours behind you."

Doc Simmons and Cole Stockton mounted up and rode out through the wilds toward the James' homestead.

After nearly four hours of slow travel through the thickest brush, pine, and aspen stands, they rode into the farm yard, and hailed the house. Charlie James threw open the door with a great big grin on his face. "Doc! You are just in time. Hanna is sweating something fierce. She is complaining of pains only about two minutes apart. Lord Almighty, I was praying that you would get here in time."

"All right, Charlie. Go and get a good fire going in that there stove. Boil me up at least four gallons of hot water. W-e-l-l, don't just stand there. Go and do it. I will be in directly. Don't worry, Hanna has got at least a few minutes before she delivers."

Charlie James turned and dashed into his cabin.

Doc Simmons turned to look at Cole Stockton. He had a wide grin on his face. "Well, that will keep Charlie occupied for a while. You know, Cole, it always amazes me. In one day, so many die, yet so many are born. One day, Cole, people won't have to wonder if the doctor will be there. It is because of men like you that someday people won't have to fear those that would harm them. I respect you a hell-of-a-lot."

"No, Sir, I respect you. If it weren't for doctors I probably wouldn't be here today. Go, Doc, tend to Hanna. Bring that new child into this world."

Doc Simmons dismounted and entered the cabin.

Cole Stockton wearily dismounted from Warrior. He stripped off his saddle, blanket, halter and other gear. He told Warrior to go and roll in the tall grass. He sat down on the porch steps and rolled himself a smoke, then lit it."

Charlie suddenly appeared in the doorway. "Brought you a cup of coffee, Marshal. It's pretty strong."

"Charlie, the stronger the better."

Chapter Seventeen

Wells Fargo

Smokey Joe Walker stepped into Wells Fargo Chief Agent Dean Myer's office, "You wanted to see me, Boss?"

"Yes, I do. Have a seat, Smokey Joe."

Smokey Joe Walker looked intently at the Chief Agent and swallowed a bit hard. He hung his head slightly, then shuffled to the chair facing the Chief Agent's desk.

"What's this all about, Chief?"

"Well, Smokey Joe, there are some that say that you have gotten too old to ride the trains. There are some that say that your eyesight has gotten so poor that you can't shoot straight any more. There are some that say that what this company needs are younger men, men that can ride the rails, ride a horse, shoot straight, and not be a burden to look out for."

"Is that what I am now, Chief? A burden? Well, now I'll save you the trouble of firing me. I quit. I'll find work elsewhere--just you wait and see."

"Wait a minute, Joe. You are not being fired. We want to retire you. There is a pension involved. Not much, but at least a pension. There is also free train and coach rides to wherever you want to go, whenever you want them."

Smokey Joe cocked his head to one side, "You mean that you want to put me out to pasture to make room for some young whippersnappers who just got out of school and ain't got the good sense that God put in an old mule. You know, Dean, things were really good when John Dunne was Chief Agent here-a-bouts. Since he was transferred to headquarters in Kansas City, and you came on the scene, things have been going really downhill. I noticed that you fired Tim Smith the other day. Well, I'll tell you what. Tim was damn good and that lilly-livered college boy with the fancy gun that you replaced him with ain't got the guts, not to mention the experience or the stomach, to take on what needs done."

"Joe! You are making me angry now. Don't continue talking, or I <u>will</u> fire you, too."

"Damn! What's stopping you? I prefer to be fired than to be retired. Just who do you think you are? I seen it coming. You think that us boys who are uneducated in book learning are just too plain stupid to do the job. That's it, ain't it?"

The Chief Agent's face turned purple with rage, "Get out of my office and don't come back. You are fired, Joe!"

Smokey Joe Walker reached up to his vest pocket, unpinned the gold badge of a Wells Fargo Special Agent and tossed it to the center of Chief Agent Dean Myer's desk.

"Take this badge. Tell you what, I'll give you one more thought before I leave. I predict that before six months have passed that Old Man Wells will be pounding on this here desk and demanding your resignation. Your newly founded ideas of a new breed in the Wells, Fargo & Company just don't hold a candle to those of us that know the West. I don't think that you know just what you are really up against."

Smokey Joe waited a long moment before continuing, "Them men out there that rob your Express cars and coaches ain't amateurs. They shoot to kill and they don't give a damn about no ed-u-ma-ca-tion. They aim their weapons and shoot. They don't care about fancy Eastern talk. Matter of fact, they'd just as soon shoot down a fancy talking dude from the East. Makes them feel like they done the West a favor by ridding the territory of them pesky fellers."

"Joe, I told you before, GET THE HELL OUT OF MY OFFICE!"

"All right, I'm gone! But, mark my words. You and your kind won't last very long."

"GET OUT!"

Smokey Joe Walker turned abruptly, walked out the door of the Chief Agent's office, and slammed the door so hard that the coveted glass window with the hand painted name and title shattered and the pieces flew to within inches of Chief Agent Dean Myer.

"Damn that guy! It will take another month to get that glass replaced."

Smokey Joe Walker stepped out into the streets of Denver, Colorado and stood still for a long moment. He breathed deeply of the cool fall Colorado air, and then turned with a big smile.

He strode to the Four Aces Saloon and pushed open the bat-wing doors. Out of habit, he stepped slightly to the right to let his eyes get accustomed to the dimness. After a moment, he looked around the room.

There was no one whom he knew so he strode up to the long bar. Kelsey Taylor, the bartender, nodded his head and moved to meet Smokey Joe at mid-bar.

"Give me a long, tall, cool one, Kelsey."

"So, Joe, they fired you, too?"

"How'd you know that, Kelsey?"

"Heard some talk the other night. Some of them new Special Agents were fired up with liquor and told that young new Chief Agent that they thought that all old agents should be fired. Matter of fact, they named you in particular. They talked big and bold about what they could do for the company seeing as they were all college graduates. I had to laugh at them, Joe."

Kelsey continued, "There were a lot of local men in here also——— tell you what, Joe, there were a few in here that night that I wouldn't trust to hold my hat whilst I stood in the john. There was some mighty mean-looking hombres in here that night and to my way of thinking, they was mighty interested in that talk. Listening in, and picking up details, I think that there will be some kind of trouble coming."

Smokey Joe took the mug of beer in his hand and pondered the situation.

"Say, Kelsey, just who were them boys in here when them so called Wells Fargo Special Agents spouted off."

"Well, Joe, let's see, there was——Mick Carter, there was Slim Kurtz, there was——u-h-h-h-m-m-m, Jake——that's all I know him by. Yah, them three was in here and listening mighty close it seemed. Now, Joe, if you think about it, Mick Carter works for Wells Fargo and Company. He ain't a regular employee, but he hunts and provides meat for them stagecoach stations. Slim Kurtz, well, Slim, hell, I don't even know what he does for a living. He pays for his drinks and that's all I care about. That man, Jake. Now, if ever there was a mean hombre, that would be my bet. He has a long knife scar down the side of his face, and he wears that pistola like he knows how to use it. Yessir, Joe, that Jake feller is my bet."

Smokey Joe Walker grinned a bit while he sipped his beer. He thought to himself, "Yah, Kelsey, with yore insight, you should be a Wells Fargo Special Agent. I can see you with all the rewards, and all the glory. Well, it ain't what it seems. You are right, though, something's amiss and I for one aim to find out."

Smokey Joe knew Jake. Jake Hillman came by that scar in a hand-to-hand knife fight with a wild Cheyenne Dog Soldier that attacked his farm and family during an uprising. Jake was a kind man who held family and friends close to his heart.

Smokey Joe also knew both of the other men and he pondered on that.

Mick Carter rode the wild trails and hunted deer, antelope, elk, and other such delicacies to enlighten the taste buds of those Eastern-born passengers who rode the rails.

Now, Slim Kurtz. There was a mysterious man. He never seemed to work, yet, he had money——he had money and spent it well. Slim bought a lot of drinks for men in the saloons. He never seemed to have a favorite saloon like others. He roamed from saloon to saloon and bought drinks here and there, always for someone with something to do with mining, freighting, or more specifically with Wells Fargo and Company.

Smokey Joe Walker nodded his head slightly. He grinned with a wry smile. He almost laughed out loud. This was too easy. Suddenly, a thought raced across his mind. "Someone is paying him to do this. Now just who could that feller be? I wonder."

Smokey Joe finished his beer, said his good evenings to Kelsey, the bartender, and slowly strolled down to the Double Eagle Saloon. He peered inside for a second, then stepped through the batwing doors.

He stepped up to the bar and ordered a cool beer. Smokey Joe sipped that beer and took in the long room. He was thinking as he sipped,

"I think that someone is thinking of a big heist from Wells Fargo and they don't want old farts like us around that can smell out a rat. We got us a new Chief and he is slipping his own men into the scene. All of these new men are fresh out of College. You know, I wonder just what college these here new men come from."

Smokey Joe Walker suddenly reached into his jeans pocket and felt the slim metal of the key. He still had it. Former Chief Agent John Dunne in a time long before had given him a key to the Wells Fargo offices, and had forgotten it.

"It might take a quick look into some awfully close held files," thought Smokey Joe. "I'd be interested to find out just where these new agents came from."

＊ ＊

A lone figure slipped up to the darkened main offices of the Wells Fargo & Co.

A key slid silently into the lock. A slow turn to the right and the tumbler slid open. The figure reached to the knob and turned it. The door opened.

"I'll be damned," exclaimed the voice of the grizzled key holder. "This lock ain't been changed since John was the boss agent. Ain't this fun? Tells exactly what kind of security this new agency has."

The darkened figure crept through the outer offices, opened the door to the clerk's area, and then, he stood in front of the main files.

He opened the top drawer and began to select files by name. Within fifteen minutes, Smokey Joe had enough background information to piece together a major conspiracy. All of the newer, younger men were from the same Eastern college.

He closed his eyes for a long moment and thought about how easy it would be for these men, should they gather together, to plan, defraud, and rob Wells Fargo of nothing less than half a million dollars.

"No wonder them guys wanted us older guys out of the scene. We could spot a heist in a minute. These guys want to steal the gold shipments from within, and make it look like they were robbed by desperadoes."

The slight sound caught Smokey Joe's attention, a chill drove up into Smokey Joe's spine and he turned to find three men standing behind him——all with drawn revolvers.

"We saw the flicker of light and shore enough, we found you, Smokey Joe Walker. Them files are opened. You are under arrest for thievery in the night, and anything else we can think of in the next twenty-four hours."

Smokey Joe Walker thought quickly to himself, "Hey, am I at least entitled to a quick telegram?"

"Hell, we got you dead to rights. A midnight robbery witnessed by two Wells Fargo Special Agents and a town Deputy Marshal. You'll go to prison for that. But, I guess that you could send one telegram."

Smokey Joe thought quickly as to who he should send such a telegram to. After a long half minute, he knew who the telegram was going to.

The Denver City Deputy Marshal read the telegram that Smokey Joe Walker wrote out.

PRIORITY: URGENT
TO: BOB COLE
   C/O SUMNER HORSE RANCH
   LOWER COLORADO TERRITORY

   ARRESTED. NEED HELP QUICK. BIG PROBLEM.
   BIG PROBLEM.

   SMOKEY JOE

"Now how in the hell is a telegram like this to a horse ranch going to help you? I, at least, would be sending messages to a lawyer."

Smokey Joe grinned widely, "W-E-L-L, Mister Town Deputy Marshal, you said that I could have one message sent to wherever I wanted it to go. I want a man named Bob Cole to know my circumstances. He works out of Federal Judge J. Wilkerson's court. So, you see, Mr. Town Marshal, I in effect wired my own counsel———unless you all are afraid of federal qualified counsel for my defense."

"Why, no. You can bring in any counsel you like. By the way, I've always wanted to ask you. Why do they call you Smokey Joe?"

"They call me Smokey Joe, because when I talk, I smoke, and someone always listens. Remember that well, jailer, because in about five days, all hell is going to break loose."

* *

Tommy Wagner, the Miller's Station telegraph runner, rode into the Sumner Ranch yard at an easy clip. He carried an urgent telegram for one Bob Cole, in care of the Sumner Ranch. He had never heard of Bob Cole and supposed that it was one of Laura Sumner's new hired hands.

Laura Sumner stepped lightly out to the porch of her ranch house and to the bottom step to greet Tommy.

"Morning, Miss Laura. I got a telegram here for someone named Bob Cole. It's marked URGENT. I don't know of anyone working for you named Bob Cole. Can this be a mistake?"

Laura grinned a bit as her eyes lit up. She hadn't heard that name in a while and it brought back memories of their first meeting.

"No, Tommy. Bob Cole can be reached here. I'll take it for him. Say, Tommy, how did you like the huevos rancheros last time you rode in here?"

"W-O-W!" he breathed, "Those were some spicy eggs, but they were so good. I really liked them steak strips that Miss Emilita put on that plate with the eggs. And, Miss Laura, you already know what I think of your biscuits."

"Well, Tommy, breakfast is still on over at the Wrangler's Cook Shack. Emilita always fixes extras, just in case a hungry young telegraph rider happens by. Ride on over and tell her that you would like to try a couple of her special breakfast tacos."

"Gee, thanks, Miss Laura. I always love to ride the messages out here. I get to try so many different kinds of food. Not like at home. Ma cooks basic——meat and potatoes."

"Enjoy yourself, Tommy."

She watched as Tommy rode up to the Wrangler Cook Shack, and dismounted. He quickly moved to the door and entered.

Laura smiled. "Wrangler's Cook Shack." That was the name that the wranglers gave it. Laura had the wranglers build, at their request, a small building next to the bunk house. It had a small, but well equipped kitchen.

The main room held a long table with straight backed wooden chairs along each side. A large stone fireplace stood at one end.

Laura also had a small bookcase built. It stood in one corner and it held about twenty-five books.

The bookcase held a Bible, a dictionary, a book of poetry, two reading primers, a copy of the most current edition of Harper's Bazarr (as could be smuggled out of the town's general store), a mail order catalogue, and several dime novels. It also held at least ten contemporary novels by known authors, including "The Last of the Mohicans."

Laura giggled to herself sometimes as she silently observed some of her wranglers sneak dime novels in between the pages of more sophisticated books of learning.

Yet, there was one dime novel that never seemed to get read. It remained in almost mint condition, and she wondered why.

What was it about this particular dime novel that caused her wranglers not to read it?

Laura got curious one day about that dime novel that no one seemed to want to read. She went purposely to the Wrangler Cook Shack for a cup of coffee.

While she sipped lazily on the strong black brew, she eased over to the book shelf and slipped that particular dime novel slightly out of its place to read the title.

She smiled reflectively, then slipped it back to its place.

The novel was entitled, "With Two Guns Blazing, The True Story of Cole Stockton, Gunfighter of the West."

Laura's wranglers didn't have to read that novel. They each knew him——personally, and they had each been touched with his sense of honor, dedication and ability.

On more than one occasion, each had witnessed the awesome sight of a Colt revolver suddenly appearing in his hand with the hammer cocked back and ready for business. They witnessed first hand, the speed and deadly nature of that Colt and they understood it: Cole Stockton was the law and that law was justice for all men.

Hot, rich dark coffee was on at all hours, and Juan Soccorro's young wife Emilita was the primary cook. Her aging father cleaned up the tables and performed other simple chores around the Wrangler Cook Shack.

He was in his age, but he enjoyed doing these odd jobs and such. For this, Laura paid him the modest sum of three dollars a month, which he graciously accepted. He had never had that much money all at one time before, and he felt good about it.

The wranglers would speak to him and listen to his stories of the way it was back then. He also loved to sit with Laura's wranglers over coffee and listen for hours unending to their tales of horse hunting and riding the wild whirlwind."

* *

Laura Sumner held the envelope containing the telegram in her hand. She pondered it. Cole was due back from riding the wild trails that very night. Should she immediately give him the message, or should she hold it for a reasonable time?

She closed her eyes in thought for a long moment.

A slow vision appeared before her eyes.

A man with gray hair and mustache was surrounded by enemies. They were taunting him. A hanging noose suddenly appeared in her mind.

Laura shuddered with the vision. Someone was in trouble, and this message bore that word.

CHAPTER EIGHTEEN

Saving Smokey Joe

Near to midnight, a bone tired and weary Cole Stockton dismounted in front of the LS Ranch stable and led his dark chestnut Warrior to his stall.

Once inside, he loosened the cinches and removed the saddle, trappings, and bridle from the stallion and placed them over the wall of the stall. He spent the next thirty minutes rubbing down the horse and speaking soothingly to him.

He forked fresh hay into the feeding trough and laid a couple of hands full of oats along the side. Warrior snorted a bit, and then nuzzled Cole's shoulder.

He grinned widely and spoke to the horse, "You like that, huh? Well, Boy, you deserve it. You got me home on time. I wonder what Laura has on the stove. No matter, anything would be good at this hour."

He stopped for a long minute at Mickey's stall. He talked to the black that was Laura's horse in a soothing voice and placed a few hands full of oats into his feeder as well.

"Mickey, don't tell Laura I did this; she will probably be upset. Let's keep it a secret."

The black shook his head up and down like he understood.

Cole took his Winchester rifle and saddle bags in hand and shuffled slowly across the ranch yard.

He stopped midway and listened a bit as the soft tones of a guitar strumming and a lonesome male voice sang about lonely times on a prairie. He smiled a bit. Some of Laura Sumner's boys were still up and serenading themselves to sleep.

He continued to the main ranch house and stepped lightly up the porch to the door. He entered the house and found a small fire still burning in the hearth.

The front room of the house felt warm and cozy. Light shadows danced along the walls in the dimly lit living room as small flames quietly consumed the remainder of the three foot log on the hearth.

This initial scene upon every return from his wild and dangerous trips always stuck closely in his mind. When on the trail, he could close his eyes and envision this very room and it felt good to him.

He laid his Winchester on the pegs reserved for it, laid his saddlebags on the floor next to the large sofa and stepped lightly to the kitchen.

A pot of coffee still sat on the stove.

He felt the side of the pot and found that the coffee was still hot. He smiled. He had been dreaming about a hot cup of dark rich coffee for the last several miles.

Another large cooking pot also sat next to the coffee. He lifted the lid and inhaled the aroma of his favorite beef and vegetable stew warming on the still simmering coals of the cast iron stove.

He stepped to the cupboard and got down a large bowl. He had almost filled it when a soft voice came from behind.

"Welcome home, Cole. I was hoping you would be on time."

He turned to find Laura Sumner clad only in her nightgown and robe, standing at the doorway. Her long dark hair was loose and fell down both sides of her shoulders.

"Now just how did you know that I was back?"

Laura grinned a bit and giggled quietly. "Cole, I always know when you come home. You forget to take off your spurs. Besides, I know the sound of your spurs from all the others."

He put down the bowl of stew and, turning, took Laura Sumner into his arms and kissed her. She melted against him and wrapped her arms around his neck.

After a long moment, she whispered into his ear, "I've missed you so much. Hold me for a long time."

"O.K., Laura, what is it?"

"Why, whatever do you mean, Cole?"

"Laura, I know you pretty well. There is something on your mind that you need to tell me and you are reluctant."

"Cole Stockton! How can you say that? I'm just glad to see you."

"I know that, and I'm mighty glad to be back. But, there is something in your voice and in your eyes that says that you are holding something back from me. What is it Laura? We promised not to hold anything back. Did I do something that I need apologize for?"

Laura lowered her eyes a bit, then looked him straight in the eyes.

"No, Cole. I have a telegram addressed to <u>Bob Cole</u>. It's marked Urgent and I really didn't want to show it to you until tomorrow morning. I was afraid that you would just dash off to save whoever needs help this time."

Cole smiled at her with a warming look, and sort of chuckled.

"Let me read the telegram. Besides, there is nothing I can do right now. I'm hungry. I am bone tired and need rest before I go dashing on out to anywhere. Besides, how do you know that it is trouble?"

"Cole, you know me. I had a vision. A man with gray hair and mustache is surrounded by many enemies. You must go, but before you go, I want you to know that——Well, I miss you so very much when you aren't here with us——with me."

"Someday, Laura, I will be with you always. Now, let me read the telegram."

Laura reached into the pocket of her robe and reluctantly handed him the message.

He read it slowly and pondered it only a moment.

"Laura, I <u>will</u> be leaving with the first light. In the meantime, sit with me while I eat this fine stew. I know that you have some of your best biscuits in the oven, still warming."

Laura Sumner, for all her knowing of Cole Stockton, still blushed like a young lady on the first compliment of her beauty.

She sat down at the small table across from Cole Stockton and watched as he hungrily devoured the stew and biscuits that she had so carefully prepared just for his arrival.

They spoke in low tones to each other.

"Now that——that, was a meal fit for king." He waited for a long moment while she looked at him questioningly, "I'm just as glad that there are no kings in this land, for I would be robbed of the one pure pleasure that I look forward to upon every return to this humble house."

The two looked deep into each other's eyes for only an instant, and then broke into laughter designed only for those in love.

Cole rose from his chair and moved to Laura. She rose at the same instant and was suddenly in his arms. He held her firmly for several long minutes.

"My dear Laura, never think for one minute that I would pack up and travel without at least one night spent savoring your cooking, and telling you how very much that I missed being with you. I've thought of nothing else for the past fifty miles, and to tell the truth, I could almost smell this stew all the way here."

The two moved to the sofa in the large living room. They embraced for a long time.

Laura leaned back against his shoulder and an almost audible sigh emitted from her lips. He placed his arm around her. His hand rested on her waist and his face softly nuzzled her hair. She closed her eyes and dreamed for a long moment.

Within twenty minutes Cole Stockton had drifted off into a deep sleep with Laura Sumner leaning against him.

Thirty minutes later, she rose carefully and softly kissed him. She knelt down on the floor and pulled his boots off. Then, she covered him with a blanket and, smiling softly, went to her own bed and settled in for the night. She pulled the covers up to her neck and turned over on her right side. She closed her eyes and drifted into sweet slumber.

The man was impossible.

* *

Three evenings later a tall lanky man dressed in trail clothes entered the Denver city jail and looked down at the skinny jailer, slouched in the wooden roller chair behind the desk, and reading a dime novel.

The novel was entitled <u>With Two Guns Blazing</u>. The jailer looked up to see who this was.

"I want to <u>see</u> and speak with Mr. Smokey Joe Walker. I understand that you are holding him here under arrest."

"W-e-l-l, Mister, I'm sorry, whoever you are. Smokey Joe Walker gets no visitors."

The tall man grinned for a second, placed his hand on the Colt revolver at his belt and withdrawing it, cocked it straight in the face of the jailer.

"Perhaps you didn't understand me. I want to speak to Smokey Joe. Get the drift now?"

The skinny jailer's face turned white as a sheet.

"Yessir! I'll open the door. Is this a jail break? I sure don't want no trouble——I'll do as you ask, please don't shoot me. I have a wife and children. May I——May I have your name Sir?"

"Take it easy, now. Just log me in as a visitor. The name is _Cole Stockton._"

The jailer's eyes were wide with awe. "You're Cole Stockton the gunfighter?"

"In a manner of speaking. I prefer to be called <u>Marshal Stockton</u>. I am the United States Marshal for the Lower Colorado. Now, you want to open that cell door, or do I?"

"Yessir, Mr. Stockton. I'll open it, but Mr. Myers is going to be awful mad."

"Just who in the hell is Mr. Myers?"

"Why, he is the Wells Fargo and Company Chief Agent here in Denver."

"I thought that John Dunne was the Chief Agent."

"Not now. Chief Agent Dunne got called back to the home office."

"I see. Since when does a Wells Fargo Chief Agent dictate who can see or not speak with a prisoner? That is up to a judge and no one else."

"I don't know, Marshal Stockton, but I have my orders."

"All right, Jailer. I want one hour, undisturbed, with this prisoner. If you tell anyone that I was here before I'm finished talking with this prisoner, you will wish that you never saw me in the first place. Do I make myself understood?"

"Yessir! Visit all you like."

An hour later Cole Stockton emerged from the cell block and announced,

"Smokey Joe Walker will stay in jail. He has confessed his doings to me and I want the city marshal and two deputies to escort him to Judge Taylor in the County Courthouse at eight o'clock in the morning. You pass that message immediately. Tell them that U.S. Marshal Stockton directed it. Furthermore, get a message to Wells Fargo Chief Agent Dean Myer. Tell him that I want to see his files in the morning. I'm sending a telegram to Regional Chief Agent John Dunne in Kansas City to authorize it.

The skinny jailer could only nod his head up and down and repeat several times, "Yessir, Yessir, Yessir, Marshal Stockton. It will be done."

"Thank you, Mr.——Mr. Oh, hell, what's your name, jailer?"

"Hank, Marshal——Hank Moulton."

"Thank you, Hank. Do this quickly, I would hate to be disappointed."

Cole Stockton turned and strode out into the night.

* *

Wells Fargo Chief Agent Dean Myer had just laid his head on the pillow when a hard banging came at the door to his boarding house room.

He sat up with a start and yelled out, "Who are you, what do you want? My God, it's almost midnight!"

A strained nervous voice spoke through the door in an urgent manner.

"Dean, it's me——Marty. Hurry, open the door, we've got big trouble."

Dean Myer threw off the covers, rose from his bed and stomped to the door. He opened it a crack, then swung it open. Marty Hellman, one of his closest friends, also a Wells Fargo Special Agent, stepped quickly into the room. His face looked ashen. He looked like he had come straight out of his favorite saloon.

"All right, Marty. What is it?"

"We got trouble, Dean——big trouble. We got to get down to the office and pull some files. U.S. Marshal Cole Stockton is in town and he forced his way into the jail to speak with that old coot, Smokey Joe. No telling what they talked about."

"Don't worry about those files, Marty. I already changed them. I anticipated something like this when I read Old Joe's eyes. They can't find anything in those files now. Go on back to your room and get some sleep."

Marty Hellman breathed a long sigh of relief.

"All right, Dean. Sorry I got so worked up. I hear that Marshal Stockton is no one to fool with. My God, he's killed a lot of men in stand up gunfights. They say that he can look into a man's eyes and see the hellfire of his soul. It's got to be the truth, I've read the dime novel about him."

Dean Myer only grinned. He <u>knew</u> how the dime novels were written——most of the time on hearsay, and several times on short interviews with drunken frontiersmen. Story tellers would sometimes read a grossly inaccurate news account, then formulate their own visions of the story in fictional novels that sold like "hotcakes" back in the gentle Eastern cities.

Myer eased his friend out the door and crawled back into bed. He closed his eyes and the vision of thousands of dollars flooded his mind. A broad smile crossed his face as he drifted off into a deep sleep.

* *

Marty Hellman shivered a bit as Dean Myer closed the door to his room. He still felt very nervous. He suddenly felt like he needed a drink.

He turned and walked to the head of the stairwell, went down the stairs, and out the door. He headed for the first saloon that showed light from the windows. He wanted to be alone with his thoughts and above all——to have a bottle of whiskey and a glass in his hand.

Minutes later, he entered the Golden Eagle Saloon. Only five or six customers stood at the bar and about the same number sat at tables around the smoky bar room.

Marty stepped up to the bar to stand beside a tall lanky man drinking a tall mug of beer who looked like he just rode out of the "sticks" and he thought, "Now here's is a <u>hick</u> if I ever saw one."

The stranger had about a week's growth of beard. His hair was a sandy color with just a touch of gray at the temples. He wore rumpled jeans, worn down boots, spurs, a dark rumpled coat, and a dark brown Stetson. A faded yellow bandana hung loosely around his neck.

Marty motioned to the bartender and called out, "Bartender, bring me a bottle of your finest whiskey. Put it on my tab."

The burly bartender reached to the bar back and picked up a full bottle of the amber-colored liquid fire. He walked slowly to Marty and placed the bottle and a glass in front of him.

"Count by the shot or buy the whole bottle, as usual?"

"The whole bottle——as usual, you know me."

"Yah, I do. That will be two bucks on your tab."

Marty Hellman nodded in acknowledgement, signed the IOU, then poured himself a drink——to the brim of the glass. He nodded to himself and then tossed it down. He felt a lot better. He poured himself another and tossed it down. He exhaled and then turned to the lanky man beside him.

"Howdy, my name's Marty. You may not believe it, but I am a Wells Fargo Special Agent." He pulled back the panel of his coat to reveal the gold badge of a Wells Fargo Special Agent.

"I am entrusted to protect shipments of all kinds of valuables from those that would want to take them for dastardly reasons of their own. I have been very successful at it and I am very proud to do this. I would like you to join me in a drink, to Wells Fargo & Company. What is your name? We might drink to you, too."

"Well, I normally don't drink the hard stuff. A cool beer is good enough. Name's Cole, Bob Cole, but yes, I'll drink a whiskey to Wells Fargo & Company."

Marty Hellman grinned widely. This new acquaintance would certainly respect him as he talked of his job, his education in one of the finest colleges back East, and his visions of the future.

Marty Hellman also looked down at the worn gun belt around the man's waist. This man looked to know guns. He looked like he used them often and then, looking at his silly grin, decided that he was just dumb enough to help his situation without realizing just what he was doing.

Yes, Marty Hellman would have a few drinks with this man and then coerce him into helping "The Few" rob the Wells Fargo & Company of thousands of dollars. After all, a "woodsy" man like this would fit the perfect description of a nondescript outlaw to be blamed for the sudden and violent robberies planned in the near future. Marty smiled inwardly to himself.

He planned to enlist this poor fellow's aid and the man would be none the wiser, until his description got plastered all over the West as the most wanted train robber of Wells Fargo & Company.

* *

Smokey Joe Walker was awake, dressed, and ready when the city marshal and two deputies opened his cell and motioned him out. All three were grim faced in their appearance.

Tom Haney, the Denver city marshal, looked at Smokey Joe for a long moment and then said, "I've listened to your outrageous stories on occasion, but I never thought that you really knew any of those men that you tell about. I am now inclined to believe you. U.S. Marshal Cole Stockton is in town and advised us to take you to court this morning. There is no way that he will be disappointed. Come, Smokey Joe, it's time to see the judge."

Marshal Haney could not believe the grin on Smokey Joe's face.

Fifteen minutes later, Smokey Joe Walker stood in front of an ashen-faced County Judge Marcus Taylor. Dean Myer stood to one side.

The courtroom clock struck exactly eight o'clock in the morning.

All present stood looking at each other. No one said anything. Silence prevailed.

A long ten minutes passed, and then, the doors to the courtroom opened, and U.S. Marshal Cole Stockton entered the court room.

He wore a rumpled dark suit with light blue shirt and navy blue tie. The silver star of a United States Marshal was pinned on his vest.

Silver spurs jingled with each step that he took. A dark brown Stetson was set somewhat back on his head. When he got a couple of steps inside, he removed his hat and held it in his hands.

Stockton walked straight up to the judge's bench. He looked Judge Taylor straight in the eyes and said, "The accused has admitted his wrong doings to me personally, and I will take personal custody of this man until his hearing at Judge Wilkerson's Court set for thirty days hence. I believe, Judge Taylor, that you already have the letter from Judge Wilkerson."

"Yes, Marshal Stockton, I do."

"I object!" came an instant reply from Dean Myer.

Cole Stockton turned to face Myer. "To what do you object, Mr. Myer?"

"This man should be tried right here and now, not the Territorial Court. He illegally entered the Wells Fargo & Company offices in the wee hours of the night and—and."

"And what, Mr. Myer? Just what did Mr. Smokey Joe Walker do in your office that night?"

"I——I, well, he was going through private Wells Fargo files when we surprised him."

"Did he steal anything, Mr. Myer?" Judge Taylor questioned.

"I can't say for sure, but I had him arrested on the spot for thievery in the night."

"Mr. Myer, you just told the court that you could not assess whether or not Mr. Walker stole anything. You just found him in your office. Is that correct?" asked Marshal Stockton.

"Yes, Marshal, I suppose that is correct."

"You suppose, Mr. Myer? I want actual proof that Mr. Smokey Joe Walker stole something from your office."

Dean Myer exhaled a long breath. "No. I can't determine that he stole anything."

Judge Taylor leaned over his desk, "W-e-l-l, Mr. Myer, it seems to me that Smokey Joe should have been jailed for nothing more than the lesser charge of breaking and entering. That charge carries at least a fifty dollar fine, providing that nothing of value was stolen."

Dean Myer was quick to respond, "He didn't have the chance to steal anything. We caught him dead to rights."

Cole Stockton intervened, "Yes. You did catch him. You caught him in the middle of reviewing some files."

Myer continued, "He broke into and entered the Wells Fargo & Company Denver Office and rummaged through private files. I had him arrested and I told the city marshal to hold him with no visitors."

Cole Stockton's smile spread wide across his face.

Judge Taylor almost choked. He coughed a couple of times, and then fought hard to clear his voice. He then looked straight at Dean Myer and said, "Mr. Myer, you may be the appointed Chief Wells Fargo Agent in Denver, but you do not have the authority to tell any law officer that a prisoner will be kept without visitation. Is that clear? Only a judge can issue that order. Furthermore, Marshal Haney, you are hereby chastised and reprimanded. No prisoner henceforth will be detained and held without visitation rights unless under my judicial approval. Do I make myself clear, Marshal?"

"Yessir! Judge."

Denver City Marshal Haney and both Deputy Marshals held beet-red faces and lowered their eyes a bit. Judge Taylor's comments cut to the heart and mind, and they would never forget them.

Cole Stockton again turned to Judge Taylor.

"And now, Judge, I would like you to honor the second clause of Judge Wilkerson's letter."

"Of course, Marshal Stockton. Smokey Joe Walker, stand and face this court. Raise your right hand and swear after me, "I, Smokey Joe

Walker, do solemnly swear to uphold the laws of the Constitution and of the United States of America, so help me God."

All eyes widened as Cole Stockton stepped forward and pinned Smokey Joe Walker with the Silver Star of Deputy United States Marshal.

"And, now Judge Taylor, the third stipulation of Judge Wilkerson's message."

Judge Taylor swallowed hard and then announced, "Dean Myer, you are hereby subpoenaed and ordered to open all of the Wells Fargo files to inspection by federal officers of the law.

Dean Myer turned a beet red and countered with, "I cannot honor this order unless properly served with notice from my superior at the main Wells Fargo & Company office in Kansas City. That will take at least twenty-four hours, Judge. After that, I will be glad to open Wells Fargo & Company files for review."

Cole Stockton suddenly stepped up to within five inches of Dean Myer and looked directly into his brown eyes.

Stockton grinned widely, almost like a little boy caught with his hand in the cookie jar. He handed Myer a copy of a telegram.

Judge Taylor announced, "Mr. Myer. You have just been served notice from your superior, Mr. John Dunne, Regional Chief Special Agent of the Wells Fargo & Company, that your files and all of the files on the premises of Wells, Fargo & Company, shall be open to inspection by federal officers. These federal officers being namely, United States Marshal Stockton and Deputy Marshal Walker. It will be done immediately and within the hour."

Myer swallowed hard. He had underestimated Stockton. A complete surprise then followed. Cole Stockton then turned once again to Myer.

"Dean Myer. You are under arrest for conspiracy to defraud the company of Wells Fargo & Company of over a hundred thousand dollars. A second charge of falsifying U.S. government records is pending, depending on what I find in your files. Thirdly, you are charged with conspiracy to commit false witness with the intent that innocent men should be hunted and tried for your crimes of intended theft of thousands or even millions of dollars from Wells Fargo & Company."

"I'll sue you for false arrest," loudly stated Myer.

"I have a signed statement attesting to your leadership in this conspiracy." countered Stockton.

"From whom may I ask?"

"From Marty Hellman," Stockton acknowledged.

"Hell, that drunkard? You'll never make it stick."

"I think so, Myer. From six 'clock this morning until the time that I walked into this courtroom, I have personally arrested two other Wells Fargo Special Agents. Both of these men have also signed statements to the effect that you, Dean Myer, were the head of a conspiracy to internally rob Wells Fargo & Company of over a hundred thousand dollars and blame all of it on, let's see, how did you put it to your friends, "Them blundering bumpkins will never know what hit them. We will arrange for some frontier scum to be blamed."

"Well, Mr. Myer. It seems that you truly do not know the manner of the West. Frontier scum as you call us have caught _you_ red handed and for that dance you will, as we say out here, pay the fiddler."

"Turn around, Mr. Myer, and place your arms behind your back. You are under arrest. Deputy Marshal Walker and I will personally escort you to the jailhouse. You may, of course, send one message to whomever you deem necessary."

Dean Myer hung his head for a long second. He had grossly underestimated this man Cole Stockton. He would make up for it in the immediate future. He would never underestimate the man again.

Chapter Nineteen

Jail Break

Cole Stockton and Smokey Joe Walker escorted Dean Myer to the Denver City Jail. As they entered the two-story stone building with the iron door and barred windows, the jailer, Hank Moulten, stood back and just stared at Myer.

He had always thought of Myer as a hero of sorts. After all, he was the Chief Agent and Wells Fargo was a most powerful influence in Denver. Now, Hank looked at Dean Myer in a different light. He now saw another hero. Smokey Joe Walker had seen through the doings and read it right.

Hank had also listened to some of Smokey Joe's stories and had never before believed that Smokey really knew even one of those men that Smokey Joe told stories about.

Now, since the previous evening, he had met face-to-face a man known to be one of the fastest gunfighters in the country. He was also U.S. Marshal. He had met Cole Stockton, face-to-face and done as the famous Marshal had bid him to do.

Yes, Hank Moulton was in a "heaven" of sorts. Within the past twenty-four hours he had found himself in the midst of famous men, and they were asking him to do their bidding. He felt glad. He was proud and smiling, and now he would be the talk of the town. He would stop in at the Golden Nugget Saloon on his way home for supper. He would have a beer at the main bar. He would no longer be just the jailer. He was important now. There would be men coming up to him and asking him the news. They would buy him a beer. They would want to know all about the jailing of Dean Myer. These were the thoughts that crossed Hank Moulton's mind as he turned the key on Dean Myer's cell in the Denver city jail.

Immediately comments came from others already there. Marty Hellman spoke out, "Dean. I was drunk. I didn't know what I was doing or saying. We've got to find a way out of here. We could hang for this. I can't hang. I have a fear of choking. I can't hang."

Dean Myer looked calculatingly at the man and said right out, "Don't worry, Marty. You won't hang."

Myer also looked appraisingly at the other two arrested Wells Fargo Special Agents in the opposite cell from him. They refused to look at him. He thought about them also, "And neither will you two. I'm going to kill all three of you myself."

* *

Deputy U.S. Marshal Smokey Joe Walker heard the slight rapping at the door of the Denver city jail. He peered through the window and saw Jailer Hank Moulton standing there. He looked a bit "under the weather," but Smokey Joe had been there before, himself.

Smokey opened the jail door. Hank Moulton stepped into the jail, slightly staggering. Smokey Joe shut the heavy iron door and slid the bar in place. He turned and looked at Hank Moulton.

"Are you all right, Hank? You have to watch these guys overnight. If you ain't O.K., then I'll stay with you."

"You bet I'm alright! Why, Smokey Joe, I just got to tell you. I had never in my life believed them stories you told——especially about you knowing Cole Stockton. But, now, Smokey Joe, you can tell me a lot more stories, because I like this."

"Just what are you talking about, Hank?"

"Well, some guys just recognized me——looked at me over at the Golden Nugget and they bought me a beer——each. Why, Joe, I feel like a million dollars. Go on, get on out of here. I know that you probably would like a cool beer, too. You just go on and I'll just nap here a bit on the sofa."

"W-e-l-l, all right, Hank. But, I'll be back in a couple of hours. I'll just go and have me some supper and a beer or two. I'll be back somewhere around midnight."

"All right, Smokey Joe. I'll see you then."

Deputy U.S. Marshal Smokey Joe Walker stepped out into the night. He listened intently as the bolt to the iron door was locked behind him. Only then, did he stride toward the nearest café for food.

Afterward, Walker made his way to the Golden Nugget Saloon for a tall mug of cool beer. He stood just outside the batwing doors and surveyed the customers before entering. The saloon only held about five customers. Normally there were at least thirty with most being cowboys. Nothing seemed immediately amiss, but in the back of his mind, something bothered him.

It was quiet, way too quiet, for the Golden Nugget. Joe Walker walked casually to the bar and looked straight at the bartender.

"Where's the big crowd?" he asked.

"Why, they ain't no crowd in here tonight, Marshal."

Smokey Joe immediately caught the influence of that statement and turned quickly, too late.

Four men surrounded him. Two men grabbed and held his arms out wide while two others alternatively beat him hard. The bartender turned down the lights in the saloon and closed it up for the night.

An hour later, the almost lifeless body of Smokey Joe Walker was dumped into the gully behind the Golden Nugget Saloon.

At the same moment, the lifeless body of Hank Moulton and three Wells Fargo Agents lay dead on the cold floor of the Denver city jail.

* *

Dean Myer smirked as his "silent" partner in the giant scheme unlocked the door to his cell and handed him a revolver. Dean wasted no time. He turned and shot Marty Hellman as he slept in the bunk. The other two men jumped up and were summarily shot dead by Dean Myer.

"Let's get the hell out of here. The jobs will go as scheduled, and then, we ride like the wind to Mexico. We will all be rich." He continued, "Somewhere along the way, I know that U.S. Marshal Cole Stockton is coming for us. I'll shoot him dead, too."

Myer and three hard-faced men stepped over the lifeless body of Hank Moulton as they silently exited the Denver city jail.

* *

Denver city marshal Tom Haney entered the jail at seven o'clock in the morning to find his jailer Hank Moulton dead. Someone had knifed him in the back.

A quick check of the cellblock revealed that all prisoners were dead of gunshot wounds except for one. That one remaining prisoner was missing, and that being Dean Myer.

Tom Haney turned and strode quickly toward the hotel and Cole Stockton. This was a matter that demanded immediate and forthright attention.

* *

Eight-year-old Jimmy Taylor and two friends were playing cowboys when they entered the gullies behind the town.

Suddenly, they found a man lying very still in the gully. It appeared that he had been beaten severely. Dried blood was caked all over his face and beard.

Jimmy and his two young friends, quietly bent over the man. They leaned closer to him, and only then saw the Silver Star on his shirtfront.

Jimmy suddenly blurted out, "Come on, this man is a Deputy Marshal and he is dead."

The children turned to go when the dead man cried out, "Help me! Help me! Get the marshal."

The trio of boys looked back at the man lying in the gully and then ran all out, towards the jail, like they were possessed with demons.

Smokey Joe Walker passed out once again.

* *

Marshal Tom Haney and Cole Stockton stood inside the cellblock of the Denver jail checking over the remains of the deceased.

"Well, Cole, they didn't leave much in the form of clues as to where they went."

"No, Tom, they didn't. Myer had to have had outside help in order to do this. Now, I want..." Cole Stockton's words trailed off as three young boys suddenly dashed into the jail shouting for the marshal.

Tom Haney stepped out to the main office. The three young boys stood there staring at the body of Hank Moulton. He quickly stepped forward and diverted their attention.

"What do you boys want here?"

"We found a dead man out back in the gullies. He's wearing a Deputy U.S. Marshal's star."

Cole Stockton stepped through the cell block door. "A dead man with a Deputy U.S. Marshal's star? Show me where."

The three boys looked toward the man with the U.S. Marshal's star on his vest. Their mouths fell somewhat open.

"You--you--you are Cole Stockton."

"Yes, I am. Will you show me the way?"

"Yessir, Marshal Stockton. Gee, you are the most famous gunfighter I ever saw. My pa swears that there is no one faster with a six-gun."

The boys led out the door and around the corner to the rear of the town. They led Cole to the deep gully where Smokey Joe Walker lay bleeding and passed out.

Cole bent down close to the man carefully checking for any sign of life from Joe Walker.

There was a shallow breathing sound. The man was still alive. Cole Stockton tore open Smokey Joe's shirt and stared at the bruises.

Smokey Joe Walker had been beaten most severely. It appeared that he had even been hit with axe handles around his middle. When his assailants thought him near death, they then dumped him in the gullies to die.

Cole sent the three boys to get the doctor. He sat down on the ground beside Smokey Joe and thought deeply, "Well now, Mister Dean Myer. I'm adding murder and the attempted murder of a federal officer to all the rest of the charges. I don't care where you run to, I <u>will</u> find you and then, you will pay the fiddler."

Just then, the three boys came running back to the gullies with the doctor and other men to help.

Stockton rose to his feet and, looking around the gully, found several sets of footprints.

When Smokey Joe was safely carried to the hospital floor of the hotel, Cole Stockton went back to the gully. He mentally calculated the distance to the nearest building, The Golden Nugget Saloon.

He pondered over the five sets of boot prints.

Two sets of prints led directly to the back door of the Golden Nugget Saloon. The other three sets of prints veered off toward the back of the jail.

Stockton strode to the back door of the Golden Nugget Saloon and tried the door. It was locked. He stepped around the corner into the alley and made his way to the boardwalk in front of the saloon.

He walked slowly to the batwing doors. The establishment was open for business. He stepped inside, holding to the left for a moment to let his eyes adjust to the dimness.

He stepped straight up to the bar and turned slightly to take in the entire room.

The tall, stocky bartender approached him and cheerfully said, "What'll it be, Mister?"

Cole Stockton turned to look deep into the bartender's eyes.

Neville Brooks, however, looked straight at the Silver Star pinned on Stockton's vest. The long quiver started in the pit of his stomach and spread slowly to his toes, his fingers, and then to his brain.

He slowly looked into Cole Stockton's eyes and felt the searing fires of hell itself. He trembled visibly.

"Who was the bartender here last night and where can I find him now?"

The question was direct and to the point. Brooks thought about silence, but the look in this man's eyes told him that he had better come up with the truth.

"Mick Treller was the bartender last night. He has a room down at Hodge House, a boarding house."

Stockton looked deeply into the bartender's eyes and nodded silently. He turned and strode purposefully out of the door, leaving the batwings fluttering to and fro.

Brooks exhaled a long breath. That man was some kind of mad, and he was going to find the truth——even if someone died over it.

* *

Mick Treller was snoring soundly as the key silently turned in the lock. The door to his room slowly opened and the tall, lanky figure stepped quietly inside. The figure stood motionless for a long moment, eyeing the slumbering man. Suddenly, he kicked the door shut with the heel of his left boot.

Treller shot straight up in bed, to stare wide-eyed at the tall man standing just inside his room. "Who the hell are you and what are you doing in my room?" he shouted.

A quiet mannered voice spoke, "I'll ask the questions. You just give the answers. You lie to me, I'll leave your hurt and bleeding carcass in the gullies for the scavengers."

Mick Treller's face lost its color. He suddenly realized just who this man was——Cole Stockton, United States Marshal. Treller guessed also that he outweighed this intruder by around fifty pounds.

Treller suddenly leaped out of the bed and was in mid-stride when a Colt revolver appeared out of nowhere and smashed across the bridge of his nose.

Treller instantly jerked backward and stumbled around as if in a groggy stupor. He slammed against the right hand wall of his room, then stood there shaking his head and feeling his face. He felt his face with his hands and when he looked at them, they held splotches of blood.

Treller's nose was bleeding, and his face felt like a large welt. Stockton had neatly laid the barrel of his Colt right at the point of the bridge of his nose and right between his eyes. It hurt like hell.

The big man was angry now. He lowered his head and charged like a raging bull across the room toward the lanky figure, his arms outstretched.

A split second later, Mick Treller lay half-naked and out cold on the floor of his room. A pitcher full of water suddenly drenched his body. He gasped and sputtered while he struggled to his knees and started to stand up.

Another quick smashing blow to the face and Treller went down again to his knees, moaning loudly. Just as his knees touched the floor, he felt Stockton's knee slam into the middle of his chest, and he flung backward to lie outstretched on his back.

The soft-spoken voice filtered through the fogginess in his brain once again, "Was that how they did it, Treller? Was that how they beat my deputy, Old Smokey Joe? Well, we are going to keep at this until you remember and tell me everything. I want names and I want their plans. In fact, I want to know everything about this bunch."

"They'll kill me if I tell," whined Treller.

"I'll kill you if you don't."

"You can't do this to me. You are a lawman. You are a federal marshal. You can't beat me to get information."

"You are right about one thing, Treller. I am a federal marshal. But, think about this——who's going to stop me?"

Treller suddenly looked up and stared directly into the fiery hell of Cole Stockton's eyes. This man meant every word of it, and Mick Treller suddenly shook with deadly fear for his life.

* *

Thirty minutes later, a ragged-looking and sloppily-dressed Mick Treller clutching a canvas bag filled with his clothes and most valuable possessions opened the door to the Denver jail. He was not too gently pushed into the outer office area.

Denver city marshal Tom Haney looked up at Treller and shook his head.

"You look like Hell, Treller. What happened to you?"

Before Treller could answer, Cole Stockton stepped through the door and spoke up for him.

"He had an accident, Tom. Damnedest thing I ever saw. We were discussing the happenings of last night at the Golden Nugget Saloon and suddenly, he took a couple of steps, tripped, and fell right into my Colt barrel. Anyway, it seems that Mr. Treller remembered some mighty interesting things about last night. After he related them to me, I thought that it might be a real good idea if he sort of left town and never came back."

Cole Stockton continued, "As a matter of fact, Tom. I would really appreciate it if you would see Mr. Treller to the afternoon stage toward the East and more genteel places. Mr. Treller seems not to want to live here in the West anymore. I heartily agree. The climate west of the Mississippi is not agreeable to his future health and welfare."

Marshal Tom Haney immediately got the jest of Stockton's statement:

Mick Treller was being run out of town and also run out of the entire West. Should Mick Treller ever show his face anywhere west of the Mississippi River again, Cole Stockton would kill him where he found him.

Marshal Haney thought for only a second, then grinned widely. "It would be a distinct pleasure to escort Mr. Treller to the afternoon stage toward St. Louis, and parts East."

Tom Haney turned once again to Mick Treller. "Come, Mick. I've just the place for you to rest until your coach is ready."

Haney motioned to one of his two deputies. "Take Mr. Treller back to our waiting place and see that he is comfortable. Get some breakfast for him. A man like Mr. Treller deserves at least one good meal before he boards the coach."

The Deputy took Treller back into the cell area.

Tom Haney looked at Cole Stockton, "You mentioned information. Just what did he tell you?"

"Well, he gave me four out of five names of the men that beat Smokey Joe. He claims that the fifth man is new to the area and he had only seen him once or twice recently. I'm going up to the hospital floor to see if Smokey Joe has come around yet. He may be able to provide more information."

Cole turned and went out the door. He stopped and stood on the boardwalk in front of the jail while he pondered Treller's answers for a long moment. "The fifth man is relatively new to this area. I'll just stop in at the livery stable first. The man just may have ridden a horse into town."

The livery stable hostler was a grubby old geezer called *Lester.* He stood only about five foot six in his stocking feet, but was a passel of wild cat in a scrap.

He wore dirty bibbed overalls and low heeled boots. A ragged Stetson with curled up brim that had seen better days sat slightly back on his head to reveal thinning locks of gray hair. Lester stood at ease with Cole Stockton and stroked his scruffy gray beard while he thought about Marshal Stockton's questions. His sky blue eyes sort of squinted while looking upward in thought.

"Yessir, Marshal. I think I seen that man. He come riding into town about four days ago. A mean one iffen I ever seen one. Fancies himself a gunfighter, I think. He wore his rig low to wrist level. Yah, Marshal, I seen him. He stands about six foot one, sort of stoutly built, and rugged looking. Carries a Bowie knife behind his left hip. Let's see now, yah, he had dark hair, almost jet-black. His eyes were deep and penetrating, in fact, he reminded me of an Injun."

Lester continued, "He stabled his hoss here. A mighty fine-looking piece of hossflesh, too. I'd call it a golden palermino. It had sort of an odd marking on its face, though. Instead of the usual blazed face, it had like a white diamond on its forehead. Ya don't see one like that very often. Well, that's all I remember right now, Marshal Stockton. Iffen I think of enny thing else, I'll come and tell ya."

"That's fair enough, Lester. Here, take this dollar and buy yourself a cool beer when you get the chance."

"Yer mighty kind, Marshal. By the way, Marshal Stockton, did you happen to have any relatives that fit the Mexican in the War for Texas?"

A silly, but knowing smile spread slowly over Cole's face.

"Lester, I know all about Sergeant Lester Franklin of the Texas Cavalry and the Battle of San Jacinto. My Father was there also, along with Captain Jasper Rollins. You're one of them that they mentioned in their stories over the years."

"Well, I'll be. Your pa wouldn't be Flint Stockton, would he?"

"Yes, Lester. Flint Stockton is my father."

"What become of him?"

"Well, he was killed by Comanche a few years back. Never the less, he taught me a great deal. It feels good to meet a friend of my father."

"Great Lord Almighty!" Lester's face brightened with excitement. "Here I am speaking to Cole Stockton, a legend with the gun, and he is son to an old friend of mine. Cole Stockton, I will help all I can. Besides, that old coot, Smokey Joe and I are pretty close. I want to help you track down them that did him harm."

"Well, Lester, I don't know about that legend part. But, if you hear or remember anything else, come and tell me."

"You got it, Marshal. Damn, I feel good. Thank you, Marshal. Just knowing that you are kin and friend to my friends, just makes my day."

Cole Stockton turned and went to the hospital floor of the hotel to see if Smokey Joe was awake yet.

* *

Smokey Joe Walker was sleeping soundly when Cole Stockton entered the hospital floor. He walked straight up to the old gent's bunk and sat down on the straight-backed wooden chair next to him. He spoke softly, "Smokey Joe, this is Cole Stockton. I don't know whether you can hear me or not, but I promise you, I will track down them that did this to you and they will face justice. You are a good man, Smokey Joe Walker, and I am proud to have you as my deputy."

Cole Stockton sat quietly for a few more minutes. He rose from the chair, turned, and strode purposefully toward the door.

A smile seemed to spread slowly across Smokey Joe Walker's face. The thumb and forefinger of his right hand suddenly moved, as if cocking and squeezing the trigger on a Colt revolver.

Chapter Twenty

Shipments of Gold

Approximately fifty miles away, somewhere between Denver and Colorado City, an old long-forgotten cabin sat back in the thick pines high in the forest.

Dean Myer sat at a makeshift table surrounded by approximately sixteen hard men, some sitting, most standing. He laid out his plans to take Wells, Fargo & Company gold shipments from the Denver and Rio Grande train that passed through the area. In fact, he promised these men that they could take the next five gold and currency shipments. Should they be able to do that, then all of them could live like kings wherever they wanted.

Dean Myer grinned with the thought of making it to Vera Cruz and spending his remaining days living like a monarch. He would bask in luxury. Anything and everything would be at his beckon and call. He would want for nothing.

As far as Myer was concerned, there was only one small obstacle, that being one U.S. Marshal named Cole Stockton. Stockton would hunt him and these men, without question. They would have to be extremely careful to cover their tracks and watch their back trails. Stockton was no fool.

Myer closed his eyes for a moment. He had underestimated Stockton in the first round. He would not take chances this time. In fact, he thought briefly, if Stockton were out of the way, they could run free rein for at least a month before Wells Fargo & Company brought in the dreaded Pinkertons to join in the hunt. Myer intended to be long gone before that happened.

* *

Miles away in Denver, City Marshal Tom Haney turned to U.S. Marshal Cole Stockton, "We sent those freshly printed wanted posters out in every direction on stagecoach and rail runs, Marshal Stockton. We'll have Dean Myer back in our jail within two days."

Stockton frowned, "I wouldn't count on it, Haney. Myer knows that I'm coming for him. I think that he is going to lie low and stay put wherever he is until he makes his move. And, I'm betting that his move will be on a gold shipment, either coach or rail. John Dunne just got into town to temporarily replace Myer. Let's walk on down to Wells Fargo & Company and talk with him. I want to bait a hook so enticing that Myer and friends can't wait to move on it."

* *

John Dunne, Regional Chief Special Agent, Wells Fargo & Company, looked up as U.S. Marshal Cole Stockton and Denver City Marshal Tom Haney entered the office. "Cole! Man, it's been a long time. I am surely glad to see you here. I'll tell you straight out. I haven't had a moment's peace since I left this office over ten months ago. To tell the truth, I hate it at the headquarters. I'd rather be right back here in the midst of doings."

"John, it's good to see you also. Now, I've a favor to ask. It will be mighty daring and bold, so to speak. But, I think that it just might draw those whom we wish to see out in the open. Of course, our plan has to stay among us."

"All right, Cole. What do you have in mind?"

"I want to you to run about a quarter of a million dollars in two separate shipments. I want one hundred thousand by coach and the rest by rail. Do both shipments at the same time." Cole continued, "I want the rail shipment on the Denver to Santa Fe run. I want the coach shipment on the Denver to Creede run. I intend that there will be some very interesting passengers on each."

"Holy Smoke, Cole, do you know what that would entail?"

"Yes, John, I do. Can you arrange it?"

"It will take about twenty-four hours, but yes, I can arrange it."

"Good. I think the shipments should move early Friday morning. Now, put the word through your normal channels. I want the <u>mouth</u>, so to speak, and I want the gang."

Cole turned to Marshal Haney. "Tom, John Dunne and I are old friends and I am going to buy him dinner tonight. I'll see you in the morning."

Tom Haney acknowledged, turned and walked out the door.

John Dunne turned to Cole Stockton, and grinned widely.

"Same arrangements as before, Cole?"

"The same, John. And, I want a posse of trusted Wells Fargo & Company men behind that coach. My deputy, Toby Bodine, and another posse, will come from the Creede side. You and I will be on that train. As I see it, Myer will try for both and that's what I want. We're going to split that outlaw group down and see just how greedy they are. I'm betting that Myer himself will go for the train because it's headed south, and that is where I want to be. This one is personal."

John Dunne reflected only a moment. "This one is personal with me also, Cole. Smokey Joe is one of my most favorite to work with. Dean Myer did him wrong and I for one want to avenge that and make it right. Let's take him good and proper. I want to see him hang for the murders."

* *

Two days later, Dean Myer sat at the small table in the hide-a-way cabin listening carefully to the grimy, unshaven, slender man standing before him. "Are you sure about that, Baily?"

"Yes, Myer. Wells Fargo & Company is making two shipments of gold and currency at the same time. One will ride the rail and the other will go by coach. Both are scheduled to leave early Friday morning. Kurtz told me to get out here right away and pass the word."

"A quarter of a million dollars in gold and currency, huh? That's really strange. Wells Fargo has never made two such shipments at the same time before. I'll have to think on that a while."

Jess Brady, the leader of the outlaw gang spoke up with his gruff voice. "Myer. I don't care if they ain't done it like this before. My boys are itching for some loot. We are all down to being almost broke. That last job we pulled didn't pan out to more than ten thousand total. A quarter of a million dollars will put us in beef, beans and cartridges for a long, long time."

"You don't understand, Brady," Myer tried to explain, "Anything different, anything other than normal routine smells of a trap. Them marshals are out after us and this is just the thing they might try to draw us out. I prefer to take our time and do it right."

"Well, then, Myer, you wait here and think on it. The boys and I are going after that coach run. It will be the easiest to take."

Brady turned to the tall, muscular man with shoulder-length black hair and piercing dark eyes standing next to Myer. "Well, Daggett? You look like you got something to say. Spit it out, Breed."

"You are going to call me "Breed" just once too often, Brady, and I may just get mad and take your scalp like my mother's people would. But that is neither here nor there at the moment. I think that Myer is right. Something just doesn't set well with this. We joined with him because he knows the Wells Fargo routines and he promised us the riches. I think that we should wait it out and just watch and see what happens."

Brady sneered with disgust at the two of them. "Well, Breed, you can try me any time you want. I'll guarantee that you will see your happy hunting ground. The simple fact is, me and my boys are going to take that coach. You two and your five boys can sit here and think about that train and the shipment on it. You don't want it, that's all right. You don't share in our loot."

Quint Daggett moved his hand slightly toward his revolver butt. Brady also set himself ready to draw. The two men glared at each other with venom in their eyes.

"Daggett! Brady! That's enough!" growled Myer. "This is no time for that kind of thing. You two can settle your differences after we get what we want. All right, Brady. You and your men take the coach. Daggett and I will think about that train shipment. Should we decide to take it with our five men, then that will be our share. Get it?"

"Yah! I got it, and you are welcome to it. I got no use for trains. They make me nervous. There is just too much space to hide lawmen on a train. A coach now, that's easy. There ain't no space for guards and my ten men can take one easy enough. The train is yours to do. We are leaving to set for that coach straight away."

Dean Myer and Quint Daggett watched silently as Brady and his men left the cabin to saddle their mounts. They turned toward the south and rode slowly away——toward the Rocky Mountain passes and Creede, Colorado.

Daggett turned to Myer with a solemn face. He squinted somewhat with darkened, almost calculating eyes, and Myer could feel the hatred swelling within the man. "One day soon, Myer, I'm going to kill that man."

"Like I said, Daggett. That can wait until we get what we want. Then, you are welcome to him. As a matter of fact, if we play it right, we can get rid of all of his men, too and take their share."

"Now that is something to think about."

* *

Just before dawn on Friday morning U.S. Marshal Cole Stockton and Wells Fargo & Company Regional Chief Special Agent John Dunne stood quietly with ten trusted special deputies at the train station. They spoke quietly together while they checked their gear, especially their weapons and ammunition supply.

Cole Stockton looked around at each man, nodded, and then in a soft voice said, "All right. Let's get the mounts on board and then get to our assigned places."

All of them lined up and quietly led their saddled horses up the plank-loading platform and into the stock car on the Denver to Santa Fe train.

Cole spoke easy to Warrior as he led him up the planks. He told Warrior to help settle the other mounts down for the train ride. Warrior shook his head up and down and snorted a bit. He understood.

Then, the men walked down the station platform where six men wielding double-barreled Express shotguns watched vigilantly as four other men loaded extremely heavy sealed strong boxes on to the Express Rail Car.

John Dunne spoke to the Express men inside the car, "All right, Macy. You and your three men will be inside the car. The rest of us will be placed throughout the train. Don't open that door until we get to Santa Fe unless it is Marshal Stockton or myself. You know the password."

"Yessir, Mr. Dunne. We'll hold it close and tight".

"I know you will, Macy. I know you will. O.K., Cole, which car shall we take?"

"John, I think that you and I will ride in the car just behind the Express Car. The other special agents will be two to a car. The passenger cars are behind us and anyone who boards the train will have to come up through those cars. I highly suspect that Myer himself will board at a station between here and Santa Fe. Each of your agents has a poster on Myer and should be able to recognize him. Most likely, he will be at the last station before the passes. They will have to have horses somewhere and my guess is the mountain passes before the straight stretch. That's where I think that they will make their move. I don't want Myer to know that you or I are on this train. We are the last ones that he will want to meet face to face."

John Dunne nodded his agreement.

There was the sudden call of "All A-b-o-a-r-d!" and the great engine suddenly spun its iron wheels and lurched forward. The engineer blew the loud whistle three times and then leaning out of the engine cab, waved farewell to those standing on the station dock as the huge engine chugged mightily to gain speed. The firehole of the huge iron engine burned like the inferno of Hell itself as the boiler reeked with hot steam.

* *

Just as the southbound train blew its whistle, Smokey Joe Walker opened blurry eyes in his hospital bed to moan a bit. His vision was foggy and he hurt like hell over his body.

Well, I'll be damned. Yer not dead and gone, you old coot. You were playing possum." The familiar voice shook him from his grogginess and he rubbed his eyes to clear them. He looked at the hazy figure leaning above him and once more rubbed his eyes. The figure slowly came into focus.

"Lester! What the hell are you looking at? Where am I? Damn, I feel like I was kicked by herd of wild mules."

"Might just as well have been, Smokey. Just you rest easy there now, Smokey Joe. You was walloped by a bunch of hard men it seems and they fairly stomped you good. You jest lie there and rest. Hell, they just beat you half to death. They done kilt everyone else at the jail, including that old jailer. Cole Stockton and John Dunne are out after Dean Meyer and them that did it."

"They are? Well, just don't stand there a gawking, get me my clothes. I got to go and help them."

"Yer too late, Joe. Stockton and Dunne took the train to Santa Fe."

Smokey Joe Walker squinted his eyes for a long moment. "Santa Fe, huh? Well now, is Kurtz still in town?"

"Well, he was, about half hour or so ago. Why do you ask?"

"Cause he is the informant. Someone slipped whilst they were beating on me and mentioned his name. He is the one that gathers the information about the gold and currency shipments and passes it to those that rob the trains and coaches. Here, help me out of this bed.

Get my clothes and my gun belt. I may have missed the train, but I am sure as hell not going to miss ole Kurtz."

"Joe, you are still pretty weak."

"All right, you can help me arrest him. Come on now, get me my clothes."

"You bet, Smokey Joe," Lester agreed, "Let's you and me go get that SOB and lock him up. You know, Smokey Joe, I hope the skinny bastard puts up a fight. I'd love to lay a good one on his skull."

"As far as I am concerned," said Smokey Joe Walker "He very well might trip and fall down in the street——more than a few times. I got a knot on my head and these ole bones are aching something fierce because of him and his mouth."

CHAPTER TWENTY-ONE

Outlaws on the Move

Eleven somber-faced men rode along the main trail from Creede, Colorado toward the north.

Deputy U.S. Marshal Toby Bodine led the group as they kept vigilant watch on the horizon and also the steep inclines of the ravines and mountain passes that they traveled through.

Somewhere in the distance there was a stagecoach making its way toward them and they would be ready to receive it. Word had it that there was over a hundred thousand dollars in gold and currency on that coach. That someone would try and take it was without question.

Also known to Bodine was that there was a group of fifteen trusted Wells Fargo & Company men about two miles behind that coach. Their objective was to meet up with that coach and pin between them any who had the notion to relieve it of its precious cargo.

* *

The trailing group of fifteen trusted were led by Wells Fargo & Company Special Agent Dan Halstead. Their orders were simple:

"Trail that coach about two miles back. At the first sign of gunfire, or suspicion, ride forward with all haste and shoot, apprehend and track down all those responsible."

Halstead also knew that Deputy U.S. Marshal Bodine was coming from the opposite side and that they would have any takers between them.

* *

Jess Brady laid his thoughts out to his ten outlaws.

"O.K., Here's how we're going to take this coach. Dirk, I want you and two others of your own choosing to get up in the rocks up there." He pointed.

"Easy as taking a candy stick from a young'un," mouthed Dirk Madson.

"Now, Wimberly——You take three men and you ride out, oh about a mile or so. That coach will come to you and they will all be shot up or missing, you stop that coach. You take good riders with you."

"O.K., Brady. We'll stop them hosses and the coach."

"Now, the rest of us will be up here," he pointed to the opposite side of the canyon. "When that coach comes through here, we are going to catch them boys in a crossfire like you ain't never seen. We are going to whittle that coach down a bit. We'll then ride to help Wimberly and his boys break open them strong boxes. There will be plenty enough gold and cash money for all to carry a share. We'll scatter, meet at the hideout, and split the whole shebang amongst us."

As a second thought, Brady injected a comment, "Should some of you not like our present so called partners, let me know. We might just work something to end that partnership——and take their share, too."

Several men agreed with Brady.

* *

On Sunday morning the Denver and Rio Grande train spun its heavy iron wheels in reverse and stopped at the Durango, Colorado station. Steam burst from valves as the great engine shut down to take on water and fuel.

Several boarding passengers stood lounging along the station house and platform. They curiously watched the train crews go about their business. One passenger in particular, though, paid careful attention to the train. He watched with calculating eyes, the activity along each car. He paid particular attention to the Express car.

Even as he watched, the Express car door slid open only slightly and one man emerged to stretch his legs, then move further onto the station platform where a woman and young girl stood with a small crowd around them.

The woman and the girl, both dressed in simple gingham, stood selling homemade sandwiches from wicker baskets. The guard sauntered over to the women and stood in line. He bought four sandwiches.

The observer took this knowledge and filed it in the back of his mind. Four thickly piled meat and cheese sandwiches on homemade bread. That meant to him that there were four Express men inside that car. That also signaled to him that there was a shipment of high value on board. Normally, the Express car only held two men.

The man continued to scan the entire train. Nothing seemed out of the ordinary. The train consisted of the engine, the fuel car, a flatbed car filled with mining equipment, a stock car filled with about fifteen saddled horses, the Express car, five passenger Pullman cars, and the caboose. All seemed normal.

Presently, the conductor called "A-l-l A-b-o-a-r-d!"

Dean Myer, dressed in a dark brown business traveling suit with dark burgundy tie, wore a fedora set straight on his head. He silently assured himself at that point that all seemed normal on this train. He also wore a shoulder holster with a Smith and Wesson .32 caliber revolver under his jacket.

Myer grinned, then looking to the left and right only slightly, and nodding, moved forward to board the last Pullman car before the caboose. Three other hard-looking men moved from the platform to board separate cars of the Denver and Rio Grande Santa Fe bound train.

Quint Daggett and one other of his men moved stealthily from the shadows of the Durango station house to board the Pullman car directly behind the Express car.

Entering the car, they took seats across the aisle from each other and settled down to get as comfortable as possible. Once seated, Daggett, out of habit, began to survey the other passengers. He looked to his left and one set of seats forward.

A middle-aged farm couple sat there speaking quietly of seed and planting time. Their eyes spoke of a great hope. Daggett silently cursed them, for he hated the farmer on his mother's people's land.

His eyes moved forward to the next seats facing toward him. A heavyset man in a dark gray suit sat alone relishing himself with one of those thick sandwiches. In fact, he had a small sack with a total of three sandwiches along with a quart jar of fresh milk.

Daggett chuckled silently to himself. The man was piggishly enjoying himself. Daggett figured him for a banker, or lawyer.

His eyes wandered to the next set of seats. A young girl dressed in a crushed red velvet traveling dress with white trim sat quietly reading a book. Her hair was long and blonde and held behind her back with a scarlet ribbon. Seated next to her was a man dressed in black, with white collar. He seemed to be some sort of preacher and was reading somewhere in the middle of what appeared to be a Bible.

Daggett's eyes eased to the next row. Two cowboys dressed in rumpled trail clothes were laughing and grinning——probably telling each other some yarns.

Finally, Daggett's eyes turned to the last set of seats on the car. These seats were directly up against the wall of the Pullman car.

A man was leaned back and snuggled against the corner with his dark brown Stetson pulled down over his eyes. The man appeared to be napping.

Daggett's eyes moved to the opposite two seats. A clean shaven man wearing a dark suit, vest, white shirt, and burgundy-colored tie sat with his eyes seemingly glued to a newspaper. This man looked to be somewhat prosperous, or at least a man of business. This man's Stetson sat slightly cocked, but mainly squarely on his head.

Daggett finished his mental tour of the car. No one seemed out of order. Yes, this car seemed to be "clean." There seemed to be no lawman in this car. Yet, experience had taught him not to relax and a small worry sensation began to nag at his brain.

The train moved slowly forward, and then picked up speed. More and more, the feeling nagged in the back of Daggett's mind that he had overlooked something.

He once more moved his eyes down the rows of seats. He was almost satisfied that the nagging feeling in his mind was only pre-action jitters when, his eyes fell on the last seat on the left row. The one up against the bulkhead of the Pullman car.

The man sitting there was now looking directly at him, and held a "silly grin" on his face. The man was looking directly into his eyes and suddenly, Quint Daggett saw the reflection of the fires of Hell. It was at that very instant that he somehow sensed his own life passing before his eyes.

Even as his hand immediately fell to the butt of his Colt, he could feel the power of those blue-green eyes penetrating the thoughts behind his own piercing dark eyes.

Daggett rose to his feet. His hand gripped the Colt revolver and was cocking it as it rose smoothly from his holster. His mouth was suddenly dry as he shouted the name "Cole Stockton" with a somewhat crackled voice.

Daggett watched as Stockton rose from the last set of seats. Stockton had also recognized the hard man at the other end of the car and now he mouthed the name "Quint Daggett."

Stockton's Colt had already cleared the holster and the cocked revolver was centered directly on Daggett's middle. The darkened bore immediately spit flame and hot lead.

Passengers in the Pullman car immediately dived to the floor. The young girl in the red traveling dress shrieked and threw herself trembling into the preacher's arms. The two cowboys just ducked down into the center of their seats. They'd seen things like this before, and both were trying to get a good look at the action. The piggish whiskey salesman tried to hide his massive frame but his rear end just wouldn't fit all the way to the floor and it stuck out some into the aisle-way.

Daggett's Colt also spit flame and deadly lead just a mere split second behind Stockton's. He fired his first round and was immediately cocking the hammer back again for a second shot when Stockton's first slug smacked into his chest and drove him staggering back against the seat back. His own bullet whined into the bulkhead of the Pullman car. Stockton fired a second bullet and this one smacked into the bulkhead right beside Daggett's head. Daggett threw himself to the floor between the seats.

Daggett's partner jumped up and was also leveling his firearm at Cole Stockton. Two of Cole's bullets simultaneously sledged him back against the wall of the car, and he slid down into the seat, rolled forward and slipped limply into the aisle way of the rail car. A bloody trail marked his path of descent.

John Dunne, hearing Daggett's name, also drew his revolver and seeing Tom Hackett reaching for his sidearm, took quick aim and shot him. Cole Stockton fired his third round into Hackett at the same instant.

Daggett slipped between the seats, now coughing up blood. He knew that he was mortally wounded, but he had guts and he intended to kill Stockton even with his own last dying breath.

* *

Dean Myer sat glancing over a newspaper, looking as unobtrusive as possible. He wanted to portray himself as a mild-mannered, gentlemanly businessman. He felt that he was succeeding.

Suddenly he thought that he heard several quick "pops" from a forward rail car. He lowered his newspaper and listened again. More of the same came and he suddenly recognized the sound as gunfire in one of the cars ahead of him.

He took out his timepiece and looked at it: too early for his men to start any action. There was something amiss.

Suddenly two men from the rear of the car stood up and moved forward. Each man wore the gold badge of Wells Fargo & Company Special Agent. Myer had never seen these men before. It suddenly struck him. These men were with John Dunne and even more so that Dunne and most likely U.S. Marshal Cole Stockton were both on this train. Stockton would be coming for him.

The popping sound suddenly escalated into recognizable gunfire and it was moving through the train toward him. "It's a trap," he mouthed silently to himself. "I've got to get off this train."

Dean Myer stood up as the two Special Agents moved into the rail car ahead of him. He turned and went out to the platform between his car and the caboose. He closed his eyes for a long moment, then with grim determination, threw himself off the moving train.

He hit the incline along the tracks with a hard thud and then uncontrollably rolled downward into the tall grasses and bushes alongside of the tracks. Long moments later he came to a stop and lay there bruised and breathing heavily.

Myer had managed to escape the train, and now he had to find a means of transportation. He knew that he had taken a chance of fate. He knew also that the train would be stopped somewhere further up the tracks and that someone would come back his way looking for him.

"I'm betting that it will be Stockton, at the very least," he thought.

Myer got slowly to his feet and looked around. All he saw was desolate prairie. He made his way back up to the tracks and looked in all directions. He looked to the west and thought he saw a thin line of smoke. He rubbed his eyes and looked once again. Yes. There was a thin wisp of smoke that reminded him of a campfire.

He began to walk toward it. He reached under his jacket to his shoulder holster and touched the butt of his revolver. He withdrew it and checked the loads. He would see who would have a camp out in this desolate land. Most likely they, whoever they were, would have water, food, and horses, maybe even, some cash money.

Myer needed all of that and more. He thought of nothing but survival as he trekked stubbornly toward that thin trail of smoke.

Chapter Twenty-Two

Outlaws take the Stagecoach

The stagecoach bearing the second shipment of two large sealed Express boxes reached the outer limits of the long canyon road. Steep sides rose above them and the road also was somewhat steep.

Jeb Morrison, the driver, watched as a sheer cliff came into sight. He spoke softly to his team of six as he pulled back on the reins and applied the wagon wheel brake to stop the coach. He turned to the shotgun guard, Tim Baily, and announced, "Going to give the team a breather. They did well to get us this far, so soon."

Tim Baily leaned down to the inner coach. "Ya'll can get out and stretch. We'll be here for about fifteen minutes, and then, we'll start the most awesomely fearful part of the trip. Some of them walls in the canyon ahead are sheer rock and there are just too many places for an ambush. Be ready for anything once we enter."

Voices from inside the coach mumbled their understanding.

The coach right hand door swung open and two Deputy U.S. Marshals stepped out of the coach to stretch their legs a bit. Each man wore a holstered revolver and carried a Winchester rifle.

Deputy U.S. Marshal Tom Royston reached to an inside vest pocket and produced the makings. He rolled himself a smoke, thumbnail lit a sulfur match and drew deeply of the tobacco. A curl of smoke lifted from his nostrils and then he slowly mouthed smoke "wreaths" and gently blew them into the air.

Deputy U.S. Marshal Myles Cutter reached into his shirt pocket and producing a peppermint candy stick wrapped in paper gently unwrapped it and broke off a small piece and put it into his mouth. He re-wrapped the remainder of the candy stick and placed it gently back into his pocket.

Tom Royston looked at him sucking on the candy and remarked, "Myles, you're like a little kid. You got to have that candy."

"Well, Tom. You've got your tobacco. Candy is at least good to the taste. Never could stand the taste of tobacco. I really don't like the smell of burning tobacco either. Thank you for not smoking in the coach."

The driver stepped down from the high box and, taking the large coach canteen, soaked his bandana and moving to each horse of his team, pressed the wetness to their muzzles. He softly spoke to each,

"Well now, we've come a far piece. There is a most frightful stretch ahead of us and I'm counting on you to bring us through this. Rest easy for now, I'll need speed when I tell you. I trust you, you can do it."

The minutes ticked slowly by and then, the driver spoke, "All right now. Let's get moving. You Marshal boys watch careful now. At the first sight or sound that ain't right, I'm putting this team into their paces. You guys keep whatever hits us off our butts."

Jeb Morrison put his team into a forward motion with, "Yo team! Lead out there Samson; get up there, Hard Times; pull there, Cotton. Get up now, Dooley, Yo there, Candy, come on show them he hosses how to pull this old coach. Stretch out there, Rusty. Hee Haw, let's get through this spooky canyon!"

The coach had made it almost to the other side when over a half dozen rifles spit fire and hot lead directly down into the coach. Jeb Morrison immediately yelled at his shotgun guard, "Told ya so! This had to be the place. Blast them guys and hold on, we are going for a wild ride."

Jeb grabbed up his long whip and cracked it low above the team's heads. The horses broke into a ground-eating run, dragging the bouncing, swaying, and careening coach almost like it was a heavy toy bauble.

Rifle fire immediately spit from the interior of the coach windows on either side amongst hard thuds slamming into the coach from above. Several of the hot lead rounds thunked through the coach top and burned into the coach interior to smack into the two Deputy U.S. Marshals.

Marshal Tom Royston fired his Winchester and then grunted with the slug that sailed into his back. He slumped down from the window letting his rifle fall from his hands. He took a deep breath and exhaled loudly. He closed his eyes for a long moment, then reached to his belt and produced his revolver. He painfully pulled himself up to the window of the coach and through tear-stained eyes searched for a target.

Marshal Myles Cutter never knew what hit him. One second he was firing upward at spurts of flame and in the next moment a bullet drove through his brain. He slumped forward and never moved. Five more bullets drove into his lifeless body.

Tom Royston glanced at his partner and hung his head for a moment. He, himself, gasped for more air as he softly looked at his friend and said, "Damn it, Myles, look what you've done. You've gone and got yourself killed. How can I ever face, Martha? I told her that I would make sure that you came back alive."

The coach team was running full out and Jeb was urging them on when a heavy slug tore through his body. He slumped down into the space below the high box. He kept hold of the reins and yelled out to his friend and shotgun guard, "Tim, take the reins and keep the team moving.

Tim bent over to take the reins when the hot burn of molten lead seared into his right side and he jerked back. The team was running full out and out of control. The coach bounced and lurched and suddenly tilted.

The yoke at the front wheels of the coach cracked and split. The team dashed ahead and the coach careened into the side of the canyon and tipped over. The carnage spilled everywhere.

* *

Jess Brady and his men cheered as they watched the coach careen and smash into the wall of the canyon. He yelled out for all to hear,

"Didn't I tell you? Didn't I tell you that we could take this coach and that fire from above would do it? Let's get on down there and rake in all that loot."

Brady and his men went to their horses. It took them a long twenty minutes to descend onto the canyon floor. They stared at the carnage. It was awesome. The bodies of four men lay broken and mangled amongst pieces of the coach.

They found the Express boxes within minutes. Brady had them placed side by side, then, shot the locks off. Brady and his men grinned widely, as they threw the tops open.

They stared inside the boxes for a long minute. There was silence.

"Rocks? They ain't nothing in these boxes but rocks! We did all this planning and shooting for two boxes of rocks?"

Brady and all of his men felt sudden anger.

"That damned Myer and Daggett. They knew. They knew what we would find. Let's go back there and kill both of them, and all them boys with them."

Suddenly, the clatter of hooves caught their ears. Horses were coming, lots of horses. The horses were coming from both ends of the canyon.

Brady and his men stood stunned with the next sight.

A group of eleven men came from the front. Another group of fifteen men closed in from the rear and all of these men wore the stars and badges of Marshals and Wells Fargo & Company Special Agents. These two groups of men were heavily armed posse's set to collect their dues.

Deputy U.S. Marshal Toby Bodine offered the challenge. "You men! You are all under arrest. Drop your weapons and grab sky. Them that don't will meet your Maker!"

Brady noticed immediately that there were four horses with the first group, each bearing bodies across the saddle. He immediately and correctly surmised them as Wimberly and his three men. Brady and his men had missed the sound of gunfire up the canyon as they fired into the coach and now they faced certain death unless——they surrendered.

* *

Smokey Joe Walker held up mainly by Lester Franklin stumbled to the batwings of the Bully Saloon. Lester peered over the "wings" and announced to Smokey Joe, "Yah, there he stands at the bar as usual and loading up Expressmen with his drinks."

"All right Lester, take out that pea shooter .22 caliber that I know you have hidden in yer pockets. Let's take this SOB now."

"How'd you know about that gun?"

"I am a Wells Fargo & Company Special Agent. I know a lot of things, Lester."

"It ain't loaded, Joe."

"Now you tell me. Aw hell, let's get him anyway."

The two older men comically stumbled up to the bar on either side of Slim Kurtz. Kurtz looked to each of them and his eyes grew wide as Smokey Joe Walker suddenly produced a Colt .36 revolver and stuck it directly into his ribs. A second sensation hit Kurtz as Lester stuck his .22 caliber revolver in his back.

Smokey Joe spoke softly.

"Hello, Kurtz. Nice to see you still in town. I bet you thought that I was dead, huh? Well, I am still kicking and now you dirty SOB, you are under arrest for conspiracy to rob Wells Fargo & Company. I'll give my own personal charges later. You can come to the jail peaceably, or you can be carried out. Take your choice——now!"

A couple of men stood up from the tables and moved to help Kurtz.

Smokey Joe Walker opened the panel of his jacket to reveal the Silver Star of a Deputy U.S. Marshal. "Back off, gents! This man is wanted bad. It wouldn't do your day right to be shot just now. Why don't you just enjoy yerselfs with a game of cards or something. No reason to git yerselfs kilt over a man like this."

The men backed off, relaxed some, and then turned to a game of poker and a beer.

Smokey Joe Walker and Lester escorted Slim Kurtz toward the jail. At about twenty yards into the walk, Kurtz suddenly *tripped* and fell face first into a pile of horse dung.

Lester looked over at Smokey Joe and got the jest. "O.K. I can do better. Come on, Kurtz, your day is only beginning." Lester Helped Kurtz to his feet and they took about four steps when Kurtz suddenly lost his footing again and fell face first into another pile of dung.

"Well, Smokey Joe," said Lester, "I reckon that this man just does not know how to walk without stepping into or worse yet, falling into dung. You know——I once knowed me a man like that. The people hung him later. He was a hoss thief. Mr. Kurtz, are you a hoss thief, or are you worse than a hoss thief? Are you an informant to outlaws? Oh, my, not that! Why, you might even have to eat every pile of hoss dung and cow pies from here to the jail."

CHAPTER TWENTY-THREE

Justice Prevails

Dean Myer's men, stationed in forward rail cars, temporarily froze, dumbfounded by the sudden burst of gunfire from the forward rail cars. They nervously looked and listened for the signal to move into action and take the Express car.

Bob Murdock and Whitt James sat across from each other in the next to last Pullman car. They each pondered as to whether to move toward the Express car or not.

Suddenly, two Wells Fargo Special Agents burst through the rear door of the Pullman car with revolvers drawn. Murdock and James panicked and reached for their own weapons. Other passengers seeing what was about to happen threw themselves to the floor of the car. Two more Special Agents in the forward part of the car swept out their own guns and issued the challenge.

Murdock and James were caught off guard and found themselves in between the four men. They just stood there, each looking in separate directions at two men each with guns drawn and ready to do grim business.

* *

Cole Stockton and John Dunne held Daggett at bay. Both lawmen stayed hunkered down behind the forward seats with Daggett on the floor behind the last set of seats.

"All right, Daggett, throw your weapons into the center aisle and stand up. You are under arrest."

"Come and get me Stockton. It will be the last steps you ever take."

"O.K., Daggett, have it your way. If you don't throw them guns out in the next ten seconds I'll come and get them, and you ain't going to like it one bit!"

"I'm a dead man anyway, Stockton, you got me good. Come and do your worst, but if it's the last thing I do, I'll take you with me!"

Cole turned to John Dunne and advised, "Keep his head down, John, I'm going after him. Myer is somewhere on this train and time is wasting."

Chief Special Agent John Dunne nodded. He rose suddenly from the back of the seats and leveling his revolver fired round after round directly into the last set of seats.

Quint Daggett ducked and held close to the floor with each slug that tore through the cushioned seats in front of him. Splinters from the back bulkhead blossomed and some showered his body. A few big ones imbedded themselves into his back.

Daggett knew immediately that Stockton was coming for him and cursed loudly. He tried to shelter himself from the splinters and line his Colt toward Stockton, but he instinctively ducked each time one of John Dunne's slugs smacked through the seats and into the wall behind him.

Suddenly, the firing stopped and Quint Daggett looked up——straight into the deadly bore of Cole Stockton's Colt. The hammer was cocked back and ready. He looked up with a pain-wracked face directly into Stockton's eyes. There was no mercy, only the reflection of Hell's fires.

Quint Daggett sighed and dropped his Colt. He rolled over on to his back and coughed blood once again.

"You got me, Stockton. You got me good. Well, better you than some tinhorn out for a reputation. At least I know that I was taken by the best. I guess that I've always known it."

Daggett struggled for breath. He coughed once again, violently. His mouth frothed with crimson and he turned over to gasp his last breath and pass into the world of a higher court's justice.

Stockton stood in silence for a long moment. John Dunne approached him and looked down at Daggett, "He was a tough man, Cole. He died hard."

Cole Stockton nodded, "All right, let's go and get Myer."

The two men moved with purpose through the cars toward the rear of the train. In each Pullman car the story was the same. John Dunne's Special Agents had the other men subdued and handcuffed. No one seemed to have encountered Dean Myer.

Cole Stockton and John Dunne searched to the very last car of the train. Even the train crew in the caboose had not seen him, <u>maybe</u>.

One crewman hung his head for a moment reflecting.

"Mr. Dunne, Marshal Stockton. Maybe I saw something, maybe I didn't."

"What is your name and what do you think you saw?" asked John Dunne.

"The name's Danford, Sir. Well, Sir, I was standing on the rear platform of the caboose and relieving myself on the tracks behind us. Just as I was closing up, looking down you understand, I thought that I saw something flash past me. I looked up, but whatever it was had disappeared. I didn't see no reason to stop the train because I thought that I was just seeing things. Well, to tell the truth, I had a bottle of whiskey with me and had taken a few snorts. Yessir, I knew it was against company policy and I'm really sorry about that. But, I have to be honest. I'm not a liar."

John Dunne turned to Cole Stockton, "Well, Cole. What do you think?"

"John, I think that this man saw Myer. I think that Myer heard the firing from up front and figured out the scheme. I think he jumped from the train and is back there somewhere. This man told us the truth, John. See that he keeps his job. Now, let's stop the train. I'm riding back there and track him down."

John Dunne turned to Danford, "You could have said nothing, but you spoke the truth. Nothing will be said or done about your infraction of the rules, this time. The rules are made for safety reasons. Your safety to be exact. Keep the rules from now on, Mr. Danford."

"Yessir. I will."

"Cole, we can mount ten men to ride with you."

"No, John. You take care of the details of the men that we got. Tracking down Myer is my job. I'll see you back in Denver."

* *

The Denver to Santa Fe train ground its heavy iron wheels to a stop.

Two trainmen opened the doors of the stock car and slid the loading platform to the ground.

Cole Stockton led Warrior out of the car and swung into the saddle. John Dunne reached up and handed him an extra canteen of water. He also gave him a small sack of oats, as well as another small sack that held a brick of cheese, home baked bread, and a quarter pound of jerky.

"I guess that you will be needing this more than us, Cole. Good Luck."

Cole Stockton stuffed the provisions into his saddlebags, then, waved to John Dunne and the trainmen as he turned Warrior toward the way that they had come and pointed him down over the track bed.

Once on more solid ground, he moved Warrior into a fast trot. The dark chestnut with blazed face seemed anxious to travel. There would be only two more hours of daylight at most.

* *

Dean Myer made his way over the five miles to reach the point from where the trail of smoke came. He lay down within the heavy brush while he looked the camp over. He smiled to himself.

He saw a team of four draw horses picketed beside a decent looking dark bay saddle horse. Several cows grazed nearby. A single covered wagon stood still amidst a cook fire. A young man and woman sat near it. They appeared to be eating an afternoon meal. He crept closer, staying near the ground. He watched them silently while his mind churned with evil thoughts. He moved silently to within thirty yards of the young couple.

Suddenly, Dean Myer stood up. He drew his revolver from his shoulder holster and shot the young man twice. The woman screamed and bent over her man.

Myer rushed forward. He grabbed up the young woman and held her in a muscular tight grip. He shot the young man again———right between the eyes.

Unable to bear the murder of her husband, the woman fainted. Dean Myer let her drop to the ground and then took off his jacket. He knelt beside the woman and began to tear her clothes off.

He was almost in the throes of taking her when she opened her eyes and began screaming again. He smashed his fist into her mouth. She kept screaming. He smashed her again and again until she only grunted as he violently took her.

Once satisfied, he slowly dressed. He put his shoulder holster on and, once again withdrawing the revolver, shot the naked woman in the head.

He then sat down and ravenously devoured the remainder of the young couple's food. When he was finished, he ransacked the wagon, finding a total of two hundred dollars in cash money.

"It isn't much, but I need it to get away from this country."

He walked to the dark bay and saddled it. He mounted, turned the horse with no remorse and rode away, leaving everything as it was.

* *

The next day around ten in the morning, Cole Stockton found Dean Myer's trail leading from the rail tracks. He pointed Warrior in the direction and followed.

Even before he got there, he could smell death in his nostrils. He looked to the sky and saw the scavengers riding low in the sky. They banked and swooped toward a landing. Stockton reached back and withdrew his Winchester. He levered a round into the chamber, lined up and followed the dive of the first vulture. He squeezed the trigger.

A split second later, the large bird seemed to twist violently, then it fell straight down in a flopping swirl. The other birds of prey followed it.

Stockton touched Warrior's flanks with his spurs and galloped steadily until he came upon the grisly scene. His face turned sour and he swore silently to himself. Cole dismounted and led Warrior to the wagon. He let the reins drop and Warrior turned to find some tall grasses to munch on.

"This man is an <u>animal</u>. To hell with the law! I'm going to kill him where I find him!"

He rummaged through the wagon and found two blankets. He wrapped each of the couple in a blanket. Then, he took the shovel from the tool bucket of the wagon and dug two graves. He gently lay each to sleep and covered them up. He looked around and placed heavy rocks over each grave so that the scavengers could not dig them up. Then he pondered about the team that Dean Myer left with no water or feed.

"I can't take them with me. I have to travel hard and fast to get this man and I can't leave them here. Enough time has already been spent burying the dead and taking care of things."

He walked up to the team and hung their feed bags in place. He would think on it. He looked to the coffeepot and it was almost full.

After a long and agonizing hour over several cups of strong coffee, he made his decision.

Cole strung a rope from one team horse to the other. He called Warrior to him.

"Well, Warrior. I guess that we got company for a while. I can't leave them here. They all appear to be good solid stock. Maybe, just maybe, they can keep up with us until we find a farmer or such that may have need of them. Besides, Laura would hate me for a long time, if I just shot them. I know how she feels about shooting horses for no reason. I guess that some of her has rubbed off on me, yet, I know in my own mind that I <u>should</u> shoot them and leave them. Still, something in the back of my mind tells me that they should come with us. What do you say, my friend?"

Warrior moved closer to Cole Stockton, nuzzled his shoulder, then moved to muzzle his face. "Yah, I thought so. Alright, we'll take them along."

Cole Stockton swung up into the saddle and taking the lead rope in hand, led the four-horse team along with him.

* *

Dean Myer rode west for another hour, then turned south toward Mexico. He had finally realized that he must run fast to escape U.S. Marshal Cole Stockton and other such authorities.

He made his decision. He would ride hard toward Mexico. Once there he would be safe. He would get his funds by taking from people who had the unfortunate luck to encounter him.

Every so often, Dean Myer would stop and rest the bay. He cautiously watched his back trail. He watched for even the slightest trace of the dust that signaled a follower and even though his body slightly shivered every so often, he kept riding south. He looked behind him repeatedly, but saw only swirling dust devils and cactus. He rode onward toward the land of Mexico and freedom.

Suddenly, three sun-browned bodies appeared in front of him. One dashed forward to grasp the bridle of the bay. The other two dashed toward him.

Dean Myer quickly reached to his shoulder holster and grasping the revolver fired point blank into the Apache's face that grabbed the reins to his mount. The Indian snapped backward.

He turned the gun on the other two, and as he pulled the trigger, a driving force hit him and threw him out of the saddle. He hit the ground with a hard thud and had the wind knocked out of him. He struggled for breath in the dry, lung-searing heat.

* *

Cole Stockton quietly sat Warrior watching the scavengers of nature swoop lower and lower until finally the leader banked in for the landing.

He reached back and drew the Winchester. He levered a round into the chamber and took aim. The vulture slammed backward in mid-air.

He fired once again and the second in line jerked violently then fell straight downward.

Cole Stockton held the Winchester cocked at his hip as he lightly touched spur to Warrior. They moved forward at a slow walk as he watched the thin trail of smoke before him. He knew what he would find. He had seen this before.

At fifty yards, his nose caught the smell. He had only now to identify the body.

At twenty-five yards, Cole withdrew his bandana and tied it over his face. Warrior hung his head a bit, but kept moving.

At ten yards, Cole Stockton dismounted with Winchester in hand. He approached the charred remains of the gruesome figure. The stench almost choked him for the flesh was freshly burned, and he had to stop and swallow hard to keep from retching out his stomach.

He gritted his teeth and closed his eyes tightly for a long moment. He coughed with the smoke and the stench as his watering eyes searched the ground around the *victim*.

A few yards from the charred, roasted human carcass, he found what he was looking for. He bent over and picked it up. He held it in his hands and whispered softly to himself, "Well, Dean Myer. It seems that justice comes in strange ways. You, that wanted to ravage the West with your greed have been ravaged by the cruelest of the West."

Cole Stockton turned away from the hideous scene and walked to Warrior. He mounted, turned his mount around and headed home, leaving the remains as he found them. A mile or so later, he reached into his vest pocket and looked at it once again——the tarnished badge of a Wells Fargo & Company Special Agent. He turned it over and read the inscripted name——*Dean Myer.*

* *

Laura Sumner eased from her bed with the early morning gray. She stood up and stretched, bringing back her arms to hug herself for a moment.

She sighed slightly, then bending down, peered under her bed.

A slight whimper and then Lady squirmed out to joyfully rise up on hind legs and place her two front paws against Laura.

"All right, lazy Lady. You were supposed to wake me before this. You are forgiven this time, but don't let it happen again."

Laura moved out through the large living room of her house. She opened the door and let Lady out to sniff her territory. She went into the small kitchen and began to put a pot of fresh coffee on the stove. After grinding up fresh coffee beans and at just at the right moment, poured the grounds into the boiling water.

Suddenly, she felt a presence behind her and she turned.

She looked straight into the blue-green eyes of Cole Stockton as he reached for her. A big smile spread over her face as she also moved into his arms.

They embraced with a most tender kiss and he could feel the early morning warmth of her body through her nightgown.

After a long minute, they parted and she looked lovingly into his face.

"I didn't hear you come in this time."

"Very simply put, I took off my spurs in the barn."

Laura started to giggle and then burst into almost uncontrollable laughter. Cole Stockton grinned like a little boy with his hand caught in a cookie jar.

Hand in hand they moved toward the hallway. At the entrance to her bedroom, Laura stopped and looked deep into Cole's eyes. She smiled warmly, then, slipped her arms around his neck, pressing herself firmly against him.

The heat of a raging prairie fire filled both of their souls.